66MI
NDFU
CK99

**PROF. JASON CREST**

Cripplegate Books

MMXXIV

BOOK
PRODUCTION
WAR ECONOMY
STANDARD

The Northern Hemisphere of this book
is dedicated to Stanislaw Lem, and the
Southern to Walerian Borowczyk.

# Cuntents

Well here's a strange little object that arrived in the mail with no return address and no publishing details on it. Part homage and part pastiche of the Olympia Press, this is an anti-narrative in the tradition of de Sade and Stewart Home (that's me btw), in which the beginning isn't really a beginning and the end definitely isn't an end.

The narrator is airlifted from a ship and taken to a secret sex laboratory in Australia where the brain waves of nymphomaniac cyborg sex slaves are recorded to no apparent purpose; after a slew of over the top shagging this novella ends before it ever really begins (well at least the reader isn't bored) with the funerary rites of one of the narrator's co-workers (who is also the author of a notorious but unavailable experimental sex novel *Rape vs. Murder*). *66mindfuck99* is short, sweet, filthy and contains a whole slew of amusing footnotes, and its author(s) very self-consciously break every literary rule they can think of.

If like me, you like to read about men having perverse sex with androids (the author takes particular delight in describing female sex kitten cyborgs pissing in the open mouths of willing young men) then this is the novella for you. "A Whole New Dimension of Sex" trumpets the back cover blurb, and for once the product lives up to the promotion. I laughed my metaphorical cock off reading this, and I'm sure you will too...

One chapter is even a word for word plagiarism of Simon Strong's story contribution to my ten year old fiction anthology *Suspect Device*; I'm sure the Pink Stainless frontman will be well flattered. I haven't got a clue how you get hold of *66mindfuck99* but make sure you do... It is a corker.... in fact the best piece of fiction I've read since erm, Snowbooks published my novel *Memphis Underground* earlier this year...

Stewart Home,<br>London<br>16 October 2007

Just got me a copy of *66mindfuck99*, a new novella by Jason Crest. It came in the post yesterday. It's a wildly incoherent tale of sexology, international travel and the mathematics of identity. I'm obviously on someone's mailing list, although the author's package was not labelled with a return address. So I've no idea where this came from. It appears to be a self-published work as there are no publisher's details anywhere within. The colour photocopied dust-jacket is very prettily done. In *66mindfuck99*, surely we are presented with a mystery wrapped in an enema.

I always wondered where the band responsible for the awesome tune, "Black Mass", got their name from and now I know. The bibliography at this novella's rear tells me Jason Crest was a mid-60s writer on literary erotica. Intriguingly, it also cites Posh Boy Records, Bryon Gysin, Ian Fleming, Isaac Asimov and Alan Turing as textual references.

I'm not sure whether the Jason Crest who wrote this is the same Jason Crest who was published by the British Journal of Experimental Literature in 1966. In fact, I don't give a monkey's. I want my bookshelves filled with recognisably experimental literature, and this fits the bill very nicely. It's so literary, in fact, that it mentions a cunt, lady-juice or a spouting cock at least on every other page. The world we thought we had lost is with us once more. No longer do we have to raise our faces expectantly to receive anaemic offerings from the likes of Eggers, Self or the rest. Here's some good gravy worth slurping!

In other news, it may delight the publishers of *66mindfuck99* to hear that the well-known Brighton mobile phone retailed, King of GSM, has opened an outlet on St James's Street.

Thuh RockHunter
Hove, 2007

# I

# SOMETIMES A CIGAR IS JUST A CIGAR BUT A ZEPPELIN IS NEVER JUST A ZEPPELIN

Les sciences ont deux extrémités qui se touchent.
La première est l'ignorance où se trouvent les
hommes en naissant. La deuxième est celle
qu'atteignent les grandes âmes.

— *the Comte de Lautréamont*

La chair des femmes a toujours occupé, sans
doute, une grande place dans mes rêves. Même à
l'état de veille, ses images ne cessent de
m'assaillir.

— *Alain Robbe-Grillet*

TIME WAS WHEN THE SKY was packed with sex and violence every night — the violence I could take or leave, but the sex was something else.

I refer of course to the constellations: star doodles of ancient filthiness, like gods morphing into beasts the better to seduce saucy goddess types and begetting monstrous offspring. You could get away with murder back in the day.

I'm still unsure whether it's unusual to be introduced to sex through a telescope. Like most young men back then, my interest in astronomy pre-dated any inkling of sex, but it must surely have been unusual in becoming its crucial catalyst. My birthday of majority fell during a sporadic astronomy phase which coincided with a parental win on the Premium Bonds that caused my generally impoverished family to grace me with a sizeable telescope. They thought it would be educational, and they were proved to be correct. I couldn't use it in the garden because the neighbours and their kids would take the piss and use it as a pretext to give me a kicking, not that they needed one, so it stayed in the corner of my bedroom like a status symbol or a conversation piece, except that I didn't know anyone to impress or even talk to. Occasionally I'd try and spy on the neighbours with it, but only the house opposite afforded any kind of view and it was unoccupied. Until one day some people moved in and the whole world of sex revealed itself to me, in the blink of an eye. The first thing I noticed was our new neighbours brought with  them a way way foxy daughter. The second that she was fortunately old enough to land a role in a book like this without getting me in too much trouble. And the third was that they had enough good sense to give her the room that afforded me the best view. I never knew her name but she had auburn hair so I'll refer to her as A---. That first day I spent an inordinately long time with my eye to its piece but there wasn't any real action till the next morning.

A--- was busy unpacking her stuff out of tea chests: teen-pulp novels, LPs & 45s, filmstar posters, files of schoolwork. She was wearing jeans and a T-shirt and I was getting some good mileage from zooming in on her burgeoning cleavage. Her mother came in the room, she was a girl from the estate who would have been contemporaneous with A---, although  blonde, so I'll call her B---. The introductions complete, the mother left the room.

B--- started helping A--- unpack but when she got to this one particular box A--- jumped in and took her arm to stop her, then she thought better of it and just shrugged and stood back while B--- took off the lid.

When B--- saw what was inside she laughed and kind of tossed her hair. She took out a pile of magazines and I zoomed in on the top one, it was called *International Sex* in a horrible sub-70s typeface and the cover was a photo of half a dozen couples copulating in a field. B--- had obviously never seen anything like it before and looked thoroughly inquisitive as she sat down on the bed and started leafing through. The first story was snappily titled "Blanche and Kerri share there [sic] sexy secret".

A--- pointed out a detail in one of the photos, a blatant pretext to sit down close to her new friend. B--- squinted up close at the magazine and nodded something. It wasn't clear whether Blanche or her friend was the subject of the discussion because their identities were ambiguous or better yet irrelevant. I gathered the thing was that one of the girls' pubises was shaved and this obviously intrigued B---. She seemed to be mildly concerned about having too much hair there and, as if to reassure her, A--- got up and kicked off her shoes and started to pull down her jeans. As the black cotton pants were revealed B--- realised what was happening and was seized by a fit of embarrassed giggles. Too late! A--- adeptly discarded the trousers and immediately took charge of situation. Brusquely seizing B---'s shoulders and turning her to face her, she forced B---'s lips open with her mouth and started to deep-tongue the poor astonished girl. B--- made a gallant but feeble attempt to deny her own urges while her hands were already exploring the secret world under her friend's T-shirt. A--- quickly became impatient and pulled the interfering garment over her head, shaking free her long hair as she discarded it. She wore no brassiere and her small breasts quivered with surprise at their release, the nipples already budding to erectness. She took a moment to remove her socks while B--- sat back bashfully with her hand over her mouth. Then A moved in and placed B---'s hands on her breasts, showing her how to agitate the nipples to best effect before recommencing their osculations.

When B--- was visibly starting to respond, A--- moved her own hands down and smoothly slid out of her pants. Spreading her thighs, she pushed B---'s hand down to her crotch and illustrated the kind of motion required there. Her cunt was spectacular, garnished as it was with a delicately topiaried thatch of auburn, the labia were long and dark while the entrance to her vagina was a contrasting pink. As B--- continued to stimulate her I could discern a thick channel of girl-essence welling up out of her depths and running down into the puckered circle of her anus. B---'s attention was now held firmly as A--- shifted emphasis to her friend. Still tonguing her, she unzipped the back of her dress. It fell away like a shell and B--- stood up momentarily to step out of it without interrupting her neolagnic ministrations to A---.

Notwithstanding her youth, B--- evidently paid a good deal of attention to her lingerie. She was elegantly attired in a bottle-green satinesque ensemble with stockings held up by a garter belt. The framework of straps and panels formed an elaborate fabric superstructure over her lihe young body. Usually concealed beneath the outer layer of clothing, this was the occult architecture of the female form— and A--- wasted little time on its demolition! Popping her new friend's pert breasts free of their encumbrance, revealing the nipples a pale tan and quite wide, but I didn't get much of an eyeful before A--- obscured them with her mouth for a couple of minutes. They reappeared darker and less wide though much longer. I assumed that A--- had been distracted by something happening in her nether regions since she was thrashing her head violently from side to side. At this point B--- removed her hand from where it had been all this time, it was slick with juices. B--- giggled something as she rubbed the fluid into A---'s taut breasts paying particular attention to the nipples, before licking it off again, to A---'s obvious delight.

B--- lay back on the bed and pulled her own scanties down, experiencing a moment of resistance as they stuck in her moistness. Then A--- nestled her head in B---'s crotch, simultaneously pulling her legs apart. The pubic hair, being blond, appeared sparse at this distance. A---'s tongue flicked carefully at the girl's clitoris, I could see it engorging as I watched, so could A--- and the sight spurred her on to new levels of ecstasy. As B---'s cunt lubricated liberally, A--- supped deliriously from the flood and her hair stuck to her face where it smeared. B--- started to thrash wildly but still she managed to manoeuvre A---'s hindquarters around so that they were sixty-nined, and then she stuck her tongue in her cunt. All the time her hands explored A---'s body, whose nipples had grown hard as nuts. A---'s hands, which had been caressing her friend's thighs, now moved in closer to the entrance of her vagina and as B--- approached orgasm A--- moved a finger inside her, accelerating the inevitable. Another finger slipped into her anus and B--- contorted beneath her, her cunt gushing. It was all too much for A--- who experienced synorgasmia, her bucking rump crashing down on her friend's face.

After lying like that for a moment, A--- extracted her fingers from her friend and squirmed about-face. B---'s face was smeared with blood from her superficially wounded nose and her lovely hair was matted likewise. A--- licked the worst of it off like something out of a wildlife documentary, then they were kissing and I remember thinking that the elixir of blood, saliva and vaginal secretions must indeed have been a heady one.

DIGRESSIVE ANECDOTE, Mr... I'm sorry I didn't get the name... most stimulating though..." remarked the recruiting officer as he shifted tellingly in his chair and straightened the razor-sharp creases in his trousers, "but do enlighten me, what was your favourite constellation?"

"Oh, Andromeda, of course, the Chained Maiden*, except she didn't look much like that to my young

---

* In classical mythology, Andromeda was the daughter of King Cepheus and Queen Cassiopeia, rulers of Joppa, a Phoenician city north-east of Egypt. She achieved immortal celebrity when the foolish queen boasted that her daughter was more beautiful than the Nereids, daughters of Nereus, the prophetic old man of the sea. The sea-nymphs overheard Cassiopeia's insult and complained to Poseidon, brother of Zeus and Hades. By way of revenge, the irascible god of the sea sent a raging flood and a monster to devastate their kingdom. Cepheus consulted with the Oracle and was advised that the only way to save the kingdom was to sacrifice Andromeda to the monster. An angry mob of subjects called for the sacrifice and the King and Queen complied, watching powerless as Andromeda was chained to the rocks, naked but for her royal jewellery, to await the approach of the monster. Fortunately, it was at this moment that Perseus passed by, returning from slaying the gorgon, Medusa. He carried with

eyes, naïve of constellations and maidens alike. But I'd been inspired by the convenience of locating her mother˙ and had devised my own mnemonic system so that I could identify other common constellations

---

him the severed head of the creature, so hideous that all who gazed upon it were turned to stone. Perseus was overwhelmed by the sacrificial victim's loveliness and agreed to rescue her in return for her hand in marriage. The parents agreed and Perseus swiftly beheaded the monster. Andromeda insisted on honoring the pact but Cassiopeia conspired with Poseidon's son and he interrupted the wedding with armed troops in an attempt to exercise his own prior claim to the princess. Greatly outnumbered, Perseus exposed the gorgon's head, literally petrifying his attackers. The marriage went ahead.

Mythology is silent on the king and queen's earthly fate, but after their deaths the royal pair were transported to the heavens by Poseidon. Cepheus's position is appropriately marked by faint stars of the third and fourth magnitudes and the treacherous queen is located in the circumpolar region that rotates perpetually about the north celestial pole, causing her throne to invert every winter. Perseus's ultimate reward was a very great constellation, eternally at Andromeda's side, with her depicted enchained.

The principal stars of Cassiopeia form a conspicuous "M" in the winter months when her throne is above the north celestial pole, and a "W" in the summer, when below it.

The rotational interchangeability of these two letters, the initials of "Man" and "Woman" respectively, has been noted by many observers but less has been made of their pictographic approximation to the respective genitalia of the sexes they initialize.

by their vague resemblances to the other letters. Andromeda proved herself difficult, and the closest isomorph I could find was the squiggle in *Tristram Shandy*, my reading of which then lay more than twenty years in the future."

"Well, we appear to be on the same wavelength." He cut an impressive figure in his starched pristine ash-grey uniform, there was a whole shitload of scrambled egg on the peak of his cap and epaulettes, and silver buttons sparkled on his tunic etc.

This interview was taking place in the chart-room of a fuck-off plush ocean-going yacht and I was the deputy captain or whatever. I'd woken up on board a couple of weeks previous after the mother of all piss-ups. I'd been covered in blood and hadn't got the foggiest idea where I was. I recognised some of the guys on board but when I asked how I'd got there they'd just tut-tutted or said things like "what were you like!" and "the state you were in!" and stuff. So I soon gave up and just took to lounging around swigging grog and barking orders. Right now we were now at anchor off an exotic desert island somewhere near the equator, which wasn't too nasty.

Maybe our Captain didn't rate my captaining or something but he'd graciously arranged my meeting with this mysterious character to fix up his loyal shipmate with the kind of appointment he felt I deserved. The two old bastards obviously went back a long way but only the two of them knew where exactly.

"Allow me to explain just a little about our organisation. This won't take long, but if you don't want to pay attention that's OK, you just won't know what's going on." the officer continued, lighting up a five-quid cigar.

"I can hardly contain myself." I went.

"I represent the interests of a... uh... heavily resourced world-wide secret organisation. For thirty-odd years we've been investigating various aspects of 'reality' and have managed to fashion a functioning worldview from the best bits of other philosophies and theologies. Our founder, whom for obvious reasons I cannot name, set up this division in 1966 for the primary purpose of procuring his mistresses. After he ceased operations in Orthogonal Time we had to redefine our role and we decided that serious research into this area was long overdue. We want you to work with us, to help us discover the answer to this deceptively modest question: 'What is sex?'"

"In order to answer the question it will be necessary first to understand it."

"It would be preferable though not essential."

"So where do you want me to go?"

"Somewhere in the outback of Australia. The exact location is classified, of course, but you will be supplied with the top-secret map reference presently. We chose Australia for the base since its vast outback could easily conceal a sizeable secret research laboratory, whilst its highly developed transport and communications infrastructure would allow easy access for workers and equipment."

"Yeah, but really?"

"Thanks to a comparatively generous immigration policy and the majority of the population's relatively liberal views on race-mixing, Australia is arguably the most multicultural nation on the planet— and proud of it! Australian women are, per capita, the most beautiful in the world, and this provides a compelling argument for miscegenation.

"You will have the not inconsiderable financial resources of our organisation behind you but due to the... uh... delicate nature of the investigation we cannot afford to associate ourselves too closely, or even distantly, or at all for that matter. That's why we need to recruit outside the organisation, you see, and your references are impeccable."

"We like to think that our organisation continues the pioneering research of the world's great sexologists, people like Havelock Ellis, George Ryley Scott, Herbert Marcuse, William H. Masters and Virginia E. Johnson, Magnus Hirschfeld, Iwan Bloch, Freud of course, and also Alfred Kinsey, Richard von Krafft-Ebbing, John Money.

We also believe that Wilhelm Reich's research into the function of the orgasm on a physical level was useful. Particularly regarding the relationship of individual neuroses to the rise of totalitarian regimes. But his research findings were often compromised to fit in with his preconceptions, and from very early on he thought he knew what was happening and he took the shortest possible routes to validate his theories. We will tolerate no such mistakes.

"Furthermore, you remain unpopular, to say the least, in some quarters due to... uh... the circumstances of your departure from your homeland. And I must emphasise this: if the slightest whiff of this thing gets out, you're on your own. It would certainly not be to your long-term advantage to implicate us in any way should that happen."

"I'm no snitch... and I won't fuck up."

"See that you do not," he went, getting up. "That will be all, Mr... umm... Be certain you get results or..." and he jerked a thumb at the narrow doorway.

As he left I flipped him the reversed victory sign behind his back. The inference was very clear. I would be successful or...

And with that the officer returned to his unmarked flying boat and departed for his next appointment, elsewhere on the mysterious planet. A "ship" would call for me the following evening and when I arrived in Oz an agent would contact me with the map reference.

As the lazy drone of the unmarked black PBY Catalina faded into nothing I noticed he'd forgotten his lighter. Sitting back in the swivelly leather and chrome armchair, I retrieved his half-smoked stogie from the ashtray, lit it up and studied the tiny machine. It was a 4" long replica of the R100 airship, designed by Barnes Wallis and launched 16 December 1920, it was cast in some kind of gunmetal and way cool.

HAT NIGHT I found it difficult to sleep, even after six Bell's. I was still unsteady on my sea legs and found the motion of the boat distinctly unrelaxing, on top of which I could hear a weird whining noise from a nearby island that was hardly more than a rock. By the early hours of the morning I was heartily sick of it and threw a sleeping bag and the remains of the bottle into a motor-skiff, then I lowered it into the water and made my way ashore intending to sleep. I was lying on the beach making headway into the bottle and starting to nod off when I heard a noise coming from behind a rock formation a few yards away. It sounded like birdsong but it was probably too early, whatever it was it was keeping me awake. I knew the island was unpopulated but I drew my revolver anyway as I got closer, the sounds resolved into a haunting refrain as I peered cautiously over the crest of the rocks. There was a small estuary on the other side and bathing there was the most beautiful woman I'd ever laid eyes on.

She had hair the colour of burning potassium and her eyes were green and the light from the moon tinted her skin with a sympathetic hue, her nipples even seemed tinged with green. At my approach, she stopped singing and smiled as though she'd been expecting me, laying back provocatively in the shallow water, which was black in the night as it lapped in the area demarked by her navel and the baseline of her naked breasts. I wondered where she'd come from. She certainly hadn't been on the boat, but she was certainly something and if I thought anything I must have assumed that the Admiral's boat had dropped her off here for some arcane reason.

Soundlessly she dived beneath the surface of the pool and reappeared immediately before me, she was a remarkable swimmer. I waded in up to my knees and she swam up to meet me, next thing I knew she kissed me languidly, her mouth tasted of the sea. She didn't seem interested in subtleties, she didn't need to be, for already her hands were busy with my trousers, they sploshed as they fell into the water and she lowered her head to my exposed... uh... belaying pin. I hadn't even noticed it growing hard, but as she worked it artfully I surely did then. Keen beyond the point of indecorum, she frotched me in the valley of her cleavage, slippy with briny, then she moved on to circling each of her nipples in turn. They grew sharp with such urgency that I thought she might prick my prick with them. And all the while she smiled up at me with a enigmatic expression. When her breasts were stimulated to their maximum she started lashing my crotch with her hair, tickling exquisitely, before she moved herself forward and the angry purple of my helmet appeared ungainly contrasted against the smooth marble of her cheek.

I had always assumed it was impossible for a chick to look dignified with an erect penis in her mouth, but she did, in spades and I felt the semen start to simmer in my gonads as she roved the member over her delicate features. She must have sussed this because she urgently popped the head back in her mouth, one minute she was expertly tonguing the slit of the glans, the next the shaft was deep in her throat. Everything ceased to exist outside of the gentle motion of her movements. I thought I could grow no harder, but I could, and did, though I knew it couldn't last long. To my utmost surprise, at the very moment that the simmering semen boiled out of my testicles she drew her head back, removing the member from her throat, and I came in seven long draughts that arced through the little space between us to be expertly caught in her fucktious mouth without losing a single drop. The muscles in her neck attested her ready ingestion of the load and still her anxious tongue flicked around her lips to capture any spillage.

And the, before I knew what was happening, she had dived below the surface of the pool and was gone. I didn't know what to think, a strange thought popped into my post-orgasmic endorphin-flooded brain as I realised her indeterminate age. It seemed impossible to even make a guess, as if she were a woman from a world without time. A woman, presumably.

CHUGGED THE SKIFF back to the awakening boat and asked the bleary-eyed Captain if he had any idea who the girl was. He shrugged and flippantly suggested I talk to the Old Stoker who was constantly tedifying people with his colourful seafaring stories. On particularly bad days he'd get smashed on grog he distilled himself in his foot-locker. Inevitably it would end with him getting his accordion out and singing filthy songs. That made the old bastard OK in my book but the Captain only tolerated him because he knew his onions and he worked for peanuts.

I found him in the engine-room playing a weird kind of patience with a deck of nuddy cards, the engines were all computerised so he didn't have a much to do.

"Arrr," he went, sucking on a convenient lime, "I've slept with myself my whole life... I can count the women I've had on the fingers of one hand... but that doesn't make me any less of a man."

"I never said it did." I went.

"Well, anyway, what can the Old Stoker do for ee?"

"I thought you were the Old Stoker."

"Arr, that be me, 'tis an old seafaring affectation to occasionally speak of oneself in the third person, where does ee think the post-modernists got the idea from?"

Ignoring his rhetorical question, I outlined the events of the previous night.

"You be sure you wasn't somnivalent?"

"Sexually aroused during sleep, you mean? Well, can you be really sure that you're awake right now?"

"And would it matter either way? Arrr, a fair point. Well, I'll tell ee what I think. There are no male mermaids*, by definition, so having the genitals of a

---

The English language is unique in distinguishing the classical Siren from the Mermaid, whose later image may have been influenced by the Tritons who were lesser divinities in the court of Poseidon. The image of the Siren has changed over the course of time. Homer, their first historian, wrote in the twelfth book of the *Odyssey* that the Sirens attracted and shipwrecked seamen. Ulysses plugged the ears of his oarsmen with wax and had himself lashed to the mast in order to hear their song and yet remain alive. The Sirens, tempted him with knowledge of all the things of this world:

οὐ γά ρ πώ τις τῆ. δε παρή λασε νηὶ μελαί νη ,

πρί ν γ' ἡ μέ ων μελί γηρυν ἀ πὸ στομά των ὁ' π' ἀ κοῦ σαι,

ἀ λλ' ὁ' γε τερψά μενος νεῖ ται καὶ πλεί ονα εἰ δώ ς.

ἲ' δμεν γά ρ τοι πά νθ' ὁ' ς' ἐ νὶ Τροί η εὐ ρεί η

' Αργεῖ οι Τρῶ έ ς τε θεῶ ν ἰ ό τητι μό γησαν,

ἲ' δμεν δ', ὁ' σσα γέ νηται ἐ πὶ χθονὶ πουλυβοτεί ρη .

For never yet has any man rowed past this isle in his black ship until he has heard the sweet voice from our lips. Nay, he has joy of it, and goes his way a wiser man. For we know all the toils that in wide Troy the Argives and Trojans endured through the will of the gods, and we know all things that come to pass upon the fruitful earth.

Homer says nothing of their appearance. Ovid described them as birds of reddish plumage with the faces of young girls and Apollonius of Rhodes said they were women in the upper part of the body and seabirds in the lower part. To the Spanish playwright Tirso de Molina, and also to heraldry, they were simply half woman, half fish.

Their nature is no less debated. Lemprière calls them nymphs in his classical dictionary, whilst in Quicherat's they are monsters and in Grimal's, demons. They are said to inhabit a western island close to Circe's but the dead body of one of them, Parthenope, was found washed ashore in Campania and gave her name to the city now called Naples. The geographer Strabo saw her grave and witnessed the games held periodically in her memory.

In the tenth book of Plato's *Republic*, eight Sirens are said to rule over the revolution of the eight concentric heavens.

In his *Bibliotheca*, the mythologist Apollodorus tells us that, aboard the Argonauts' ship, Orpheus sang more sweetly than the Sirens so that they threw themselves into the sea and were changed into rocks, their fate being to die when their spell went unheeded, and according to a twelfth century Latin bestiary:

The SIRENAE (Sirens), so Physiologus says, are deadly creatures who are made like human beings from the head to the navel, while their lower parts down to the feet are winged. They give forth musical songs in a melodious manner, which songs are very lovely, and thus they charm the ears of sailormen and allure them to themselves. They entice the hearing of these poor chaps by a wonderful sweetness of rhythm, and put them fish means they must fertilise their eggs by stealing the seed of humans."

"But she swallowed it! I saw her..."

"Ah yes! But only to regurgitate when she reached her nest. This is what they do and this is the way in which they do it..."

"Shit! I'll never be able to eat a fish again! Why! It could be my very own progeny!"

"Aye, ye'll always dread the day that you're served up a fish with your own features."

"Don't call me Fish-face..."

"Ah-har-hehehe..."

---

to sleep. At last when they see that the sailors are deeply slumbering, they pounce upon them and tear them to bits.

That's the way in which ignorant and incautious human beings get tricked by pretty voices, when they are charmed by indelicacies, ostentations and pleasures, or when they become licentious with comedies, tragedies and various ditties. They lose their mental vigour as if in a deep sleep, and suddenly the reaving pounce of the Enemy is upon them.

In 1403, a Siren slipped through a breach in a Dutch dyke and lived the remainder of her life in Haarlem. Her speech was indecipherable but she worshipped the cross as if by instinct. A chronicler of the sixteenth century argued that she was not a fish because she had been taught how to weave and that she was not a woman because she was able to live in water.

More recently, Franz Kafka, with characteristic perversity, noted that it did the Sirens an injustice to think that they intended to seduce, they knew that they had claws and sterile wombs and they lamented this aloud. They could not help it if their laments sounded so beautiful.

"Well, thanks Old Stoker... Fucking hell, what a revelation."

"Arr, no the thanks are all mine, for I'll be able to dine out on this story for a good while to come. Ahhh... hehehehe..."

Somewhat consternated, I made my way back on deck and stared at the wake unfolding at the back of the boat. Beneath the Red Duster I lit up a handy 7-skinner and leant against the jackstaff pondering the moral implications of sex with a mythical creature. Was it socially acceptable enough to brag about? It was difficult to say given the idiosyncratic and inconsistent nature of peoples' attitudes to sex. I mean, two chicks getting it on was one thing and a swift gobble-job was another, but this had overtones of bestiality, and maybe even necrophilia if the species was extinct. But what if it had never actually existed?

Thusly I dithered till nightfall, then went below and lay on my bunk smoking dope and eating cream crackers. I hadn't bothered putting the light on and the full-moonlight came in through the window, until it went dark as if a cloud had passed overhead. But then it occurred to me that we were somewhere near the equator and clouds were scarce. I went up on deck and the Stoker was waiting with a "bison's chair" for me, but instead of reaching to a ship alongside, the line that was affixed to the harness went straight upwards, disappearing into the darkness of the night sky. It was only after my pupils had dilated for a couple of minutes that the silhouette of the Zeppelin became apparent. Enthusiastically I dashed below, grabbed a bag and threw in some clothes, toiletries and my enviable supply of neurocomestibles. I bid farewell to the Stoker as he strapped me in.

"Avast behind!" he bellowed into a megaphone, then collapsed in a chuckling fit. There was a lurching elevatory sensation and I was winched on board the bucking airship.

ATER I WOULD LEARN that The Org used Zeppelins since they were radar-invisible and as such could navigate the night sky as they pleased. We snook into Australian airspace three days later and I was dropped on the remote New South Wales coast where an Org staff-car was waiting to take me into Sydney. I hired a Land Rover and booked it onto the Indian Pacific to Kalgoorlie, from there I'd drive up to the Org HQ. I still hadn't got the co-ordinates but I was assured they'd be supplied, I was really hoping that the base was camouflaged as a spooky old ghost town or something.

I had a few hours to kill before the train was due to leave so I went round and round the city on the monorail. It was no waste of time to start picking up the idiom: the Americanesque advertisements, the unflinchingly casual clothes of the men; the afore-mentioned exoticism of the women; the bright yellow needle-bins on the streetlamps; the TΔC road safety warnings: IF YOU DRINK, THEN DRIVE, YOU'RE A BLOODY IDIOT; the thick rash of mobile-phone towers and the impact of infotechnology on hoardings and shop windows; the cloying aroma of barbecuing steaks; the occasional helicopter; the preponderance of white dog-turds, long obsolete in the UK; the public appeals for cancer and homeless funds: THANK GOD FOR THE SALVO'S – all the small, fleeting impressions that were as important to my trade as are broken bark and bent twigs to the trapper in the jungle.

Then I realised I was bored to fuck so I figured I'd check out the pornoramas in King's Cross. I selected the XXX-a-Go-Go and confronted a geezer behind plexi-glass who was wearing a t-shirt that said "The Penis — mightier than the sword". He asked for A$8 and got it. The A$5 note was a lurid purple plastic number with a transparent watermark, the A$1 coin was like a quid but the A$2 was half the size which seemed odd.

I went through to the cinema and tripped on the way in. I was always surprised by how especially dark it was in porno cinemas and I blundered into an empty seat, navigating by way of the flashes of light as the toilet-door opened and closed, which was frequently. The tiny screen presented a lame domestically-produced number about three female prison wardens molesting a prisoner with a huge penis. One of the chicks kept sucking the guy's hairy old bollocks, which didn't make good camera so far

as I was concerned, but pretty soon the jism was
spraying all over the shop.

---

The Oxford English Dictionary has the following to say
regarding this interesting word:

> **Jism** (dʒɪz(ə)m). *slang* (orig. *US*). Also chism, gism, jizz, etc.
> [origin unknown]. **a.** Energy, strength. **b.** Semen, sperm. In
> sense b often regarded as a taboo-word.

It goes on to list the following variant spellings: chissum,
jizzum, jisum, jissom, gissum. The American author Kurt
Vonnegut has posited a future where the spelling "jizzum" is
standardized by the US Federal Government, and there exist
even more variants which substitute "y" for "i". The
pronunciation of the word is not debated, and is represented
in the OED in the International Phonetic Alphabet. Vonnegut
argues that the transliteration of this pronunciation into the
standard Roman alphabet has never been formalized due to
the taboo nature of the word, but this ignores the
formalization of spelling of almost all other taboo words,
including the oedipal pejorative. The following table
summarizes the possible transliterations:

$$d\ʒ \rightarrow ch\ /\ g\ /\ j$$
$$ɪ \rightarrow i\ /\ y$$
$$z \rightarrow s\ /\ ss\ /\ z\ /\ zz$$
$$(ə) \rightarrow o\ /\ u\ /\ optional$$
$$m \rightarrow m\ /\ optional$$

Every permutation appears to be covered in this table and
it may be observed that the only consistency between
potential spellings is in the case of the ultimate "m", which is
in any case optional in the abbreviated form of the word. Even
were this not the case, the letter could not play the role of
sole distinguisher, since any word ending in "m" would thus
have to mean "jism", which is obviously not the case. But if

The film went on for so long that I thought I'd
been twisted and there weren't going to be any live
girls but as my eyes adjusted to the darkness I noticed
the gymnasiac monkey bars round the side of the
screen. And sure enough, after Mr. Hirsute-nads had

---

every other component is variable, then *what* is it that governs
the construction of the word "jism" and sets it apart from all
other words? This is the "Jism Paradox".

This line of reasoning has implications for fields other than
semantics. Theologically, for instance, talk of the "soul"
becomes even more difficult than it already is since that which
is common to all humans is not that which differentiates us
from things not human, and that which is common to all
humans may also be common to some things not human. Let
us observe here that human DNA is equally of no help as a
qualifying factor since it is to be found in well-preserved
corpses.

To give an example: a 100% quadriplegic, e.g. Professor
Stephen Hawking, is unquestionably human and so too is he
conscious but intrinsically immobile. If we compare him with
someone mobile yet suffering from advanced dementia, the
common factors would be limited to a resemblance of form.
Now if we compare either of these examples with a fresh
corpse, i.e. a completely unconscious and immobile form. The
resemblance of the corpse to either the dementee or to
Hawking would be at least as strong as the resemblance of the
dementee to Hawking or vice-versa.

In the field of literature the Jism Paradox implies that no
text may be generated, even if there existed a universal
language, that could include the whole of its potential
readership.

squirted on everything conceivable, the lights went up and this heavy Aussie voice came over the tannoy:

"G'day mates. Glad you could make it. Now let's have a big Aussie welcome for SQWXAB-zzzzzzzt!" her name was lost in a burst of static, "and remember, the more noise you make the dirtier she gets."

There was a smattering of polite applause and a spotlight came on and the sex-worker stepped from behind the curtain. I was surprised and pleased to see that she was kitted out in an airhostess's uniform. I would have thought that this routine was long out of style, but it could have been a function of the celebrated Aussie culture-lag, or some kind of ultra-hip retro-kitsch angle, or maybe she really was an airhostess doing a spot of moonlighting— either way, it was damn sexy.

The inappropriate strains of The Red Crayola's *Pink Stainless Tail* blasted through the crackly PA as she strutted round pouting and running her hands over herself for a couple of minutes. It would be a tricky number to get funky to.

It had just started to get tedious when she began wriggling out of her pencil skirt, she edged down the zipper teasingly, her eyes closed in an unconvincing arrogant/come-on glower as she oooozed the garment off to reveal black pants and a garter-belt beneath her flapping shirt-tails. She took a moment to fold the skirt then wiggled over and put it out of the way at the back of the stage.

Things began to hot up as she fingered her tie suggestively, culminating in violently pulling it around her neck, all the while moaning soundlessly under the psychedelic din of the record. She took off the pillbox hat and threw it over with the skirt and her bleached blonde hair fell down over her shoulders, it was a nice job, the roots showed but this could have been intentional, to give the performance the unaffected girl-next-door angle.

Briskly the ecdysiast removed her scarlet box-jacket, again placing it neatly with the other items, and she went down on her knees, discarded the tie and put her left hand down her scanties, unbuttoning her blouse with right. This took a little while because she was swaying and panting as she masturbated, or pretended to, and it was with a touching amateurism that she had to pause and use both hands to undo the last few buttons. When it was off she went and put it with the other stuff, which ruined the continuity a bit, but then she knelt in her meagre underwear and started exploring her body with her hands, gently fingering her thighs, her belly and her breasts, which she squeezed up together and rubbed the nipples with her thumbs through the lacy material.

Finally she reached behind her back, holding onto her brassiere she undid the clip, the straps fell loose, she wiggled one shoulder out, then the other, and cast a wicked smile at the crowd before removing it completely. Her breasts were plump and firm, their deep red nipples erect. She put the bra aside and tweaked them, swaying in time to the discordant music.


(no permission to reproduce lyrics)

At this point, she put a leg up on a bar and undid the clips on the suspenders, then the other leg and she took off the belt, she rubbed it over her body, concentrating on her breasts and then she looked ecstatic again before discarding it. She bobbed round a bit more like that before turning her back and bending over with her legs together. Ever so slowly she pulled her pants down, almost imperceptibly, but first you could just see the crack of her arse and then more until they were round her stockinged thighs and eventually they came off altogether. These she placed with the previously discarded items, forming a stratified record of her disrobing.

She turned with one hand covering herself and the other playing coyly with her breasts, gradually the hand covering her grew languid, all the time she had a rapt expression on her face, she was showing more of her pubic hair, neatly shaved into an exact isosceles, and then her fingers were going into herself and she knelt on both knees leaning back, one hand caressing the entrance to her vagina, the other her thighs, and then she was showing the audience her moistening nether-lips.

Now her hands began to work faster, she was gasping and moaning and even let out an audible squeal as the spotlight went down and the music faded simultaneously. There was some kind of technical hitch and we sat in darkness for a couple of seconds. When the lights came up again she was kneeling at the back of the stage unwrapping a Cherry Ripe, an indigenous Australian confection: cherries and coconut in thick dark chocolate. She struggled for a moment with the polythene, then used her teeth to pull off the wrapper. Her breasts bounced jauntily as the polythene parted and she squeezed the chocolate bar out. Discarding the wrapper to the side of the stage, she sat with her legs apart, bent at the knees so as to illuminate the most shameless view for the audience. Her left hand moved downward and her first and second fingers parted her lips, she allowed them to play there for a few moments, gently stroking at the creases inside. Her clitoris grew with the excitement and revealed itself proudly. Her expression was one of the utmost concentration, occasionally lapsing momentarily as she seemed to forget where she was, completely oblivious of the audience, who maintained total silence for the duration of the display.

Ceasing to stroke herself now, her nimble fingers parted the lips for penetration. Her right hand brought the chocolate bar toward her sex from its rear, rubbing at the furrow, the harder fondant filling of the bar maintained its integrity as she drove it home. Now she gently oscillated the bar in and out. As it displaced its own weight a thick fluid oozed from her cunt, her own fluids mixed with the melting chocolate. She dipped the fingers of her left hand into the folds of her cunt around the bar and collected as much as she could, then brought her hand to her mouth and gingerly tasted of the brew— it occurred to me that many members of the audience would have paid dearly for this privilege. She went through a couple of positions, turning her back and showing us it going in from the rear, then sideways which wasn't so satisfactory since you couldn't see much in profile. Then the confection began to lose its integrity and she withdrew it, a flaccid pink dechocolated thing. Ostentatiously, using her tongue and teeth she devoured the bar and sucked the residue from her fingers as she left the stage, the insides of her thighs smeared with brown. The projector started up again.

WATCHED A BIT LONGER, but the law of diminishing returns ensured that the flix got progressively more tedious so I decided to piss off. Outside of the joint some chick asked me for a light, my eyes hadn't adjusted to the light and it took a moment before I realised it was the stripper-chick. I pulled out the Director's zeppelin and fired up her fag.

"Thanks," she went, "Neat lighter."

"Uh yeah," I went, "But it looks kinda like a penis."

"Everything looks kinda like a penis when you're in my line of work." she took  a long drag, "I've been doing this for long two years, give and take. If this mouth could talk, it could tell you some stuff."

My stomach interjected, "Fuck! Excuse me. I'm new in town. Where do you eat round here? Gotta be swift."

"I'll sow you. Why not..."

We made for the L'Oeuf d'Or dinerette and the severity of my hunger suddenly engendered a frenzy of metabolic self-reference in which my stomach attempted to digest itself. I ordered scrambled eggs and she went for chicken and chips.

"There's only one thing sexier than watching a beautiful woman masturbate— and that's watching a beautiful woman masturbate another beautiful woman." I said, like I was Oscar Wilde, only not.

"Well, you should come back for Act II."

"I only wish I could, but I gotta get moving. How d'you get into this line? Do you have Job Centres here or what?"

"Yeah," she confessed, "I do like to enjoy myself. I've masturbated two or three times a day for as long as I can remember. To start with I just used my fingers but now I like to vary it with other objects: fruit, vegetables, groceries, hand-tools, toiletries, chocolate bars. Chocolate's good. Everybody knows that eating it releases endorphins, similar to falling in love, and smearing it on any mucus membrane has a similar effect. My love demands a physical expression. And as you've observed, I favour the favours of the Cherry Ripe, the consistency of the filling lends the chocolate a high degree of cohesion and the delicate friction of the coconut produces the most thrilling sensations. I've used regular dildos too of course. One boyfriend carved me a one from a piece of firewood and I enjoyed it so much that I ditched him. Later, I found that most of my boy-friends enjoyed watching me masturbate, it was a huge turn-on for them so I'd arrange elaborate schemes for them to catch me in flagranté.

In the light of this, I wondered about wanking for cash but I figured you needed a figure to do it professionally and I thought my tits were too small. But one time I was fucking this psychiatrist, he was a first-rate dirty old sod, but he told me something interesting... not whilst we were actually fucking though, you understand. He had this theory that men's preoccupation with breast size was an over-compensation and was actually a sublimation of latent male homosexuality. He reckoned that breasts are a quantitative differentiation between the sexes, the biggest male breasts being larger than the smallest female breasts. The mammary glands themselves can not be counted as significant otherwise there would be no currency in women having silicon, ie artificial, enlargements. On the other hand, the generative organs are qualitatively differentiated between the sexes. His point was that the preference of a quantitative differentiation over a qualitative one was due to its prominence rather than its importance, and that this was an unsophisticated criteria."

"Yeah, Alan Turing, the mathematical genius, grew tits when the pigs put him on the hormones for being a fruit. Ironic, huh?"

"Um, yeah. I guess that's what he meant."

"Who? Turing?"

"No the shrink guy."

"Well, it's been good talking, but I really must be off now. Train to catch and all that."

"Yeah, well, maybe see you next time you're in town. You know where to find me..."

"Absolutely." I got the tab then wandered back to the station and found the platform, the train, the carriage, the compartment, the seat, and made myself comfy.

Pretty soon there was a knock on the door and a conductor came in with a postcard for me. I pissed around pretending to look for a tip for him and the geezer got bored and went off like I'd intended all along. This turned out to be a shame since it meant that I couldn't quiz him about the lack of any address or addressee on the card, all that was written was a map reference (here withheld for security reasons) in blue biro. The obverse of the postcard was a cartoon of the saucy English seaside variety showing two schoolboys in an art gallery looking at a painting of a nude. One was saying to the other "Cor Blimey! My mum said if I looked at pictures like this I'd turn to stone... It's started already!"

HERE WAS A SATISFYING SYMBOLISM embodied in the concept of the "Nullarbor Express". The train was named for the tremendous plain that was spanned by a straight stretch of rail exceeded in length only by the Trans-Siberian Railway. The eponymous lack of trees conjured a powerful image of symbolic phallus-lack, squarely contradicted by the crude Freudianism of the locomotive with its attendant imagery of pistons and cylinders therein invoked, not forgetting all that horsepower. This was the loco-eroticism that had been ruthlessly exploited in the great erotic train journeys of modern cinema, notably Alain Robbe-Grillet's *Trans Europ Express* and Walerian Borowczyk's fictitious *Love Express.*

As we came to the outskirts of the city the tracks carried us through a sparse but evenly spaced artificial forest and I closed my eyes against the flashes of glare. The action of the diffused flicker (between 8 and 13Hz) on my retina provoked alpha rhythms in my brain and I experienced dazzling lights of unearthly brilliance and colour developing in magnitude and complexity of pattern as long as the stimulation lasted`.

---

In 1960 Ian Sommerville, mathematician and associate of William Burroughs, published a landmark article on the subject of recreational flicker machines. He suggested that the work of abstract painters such as Klee and Miró was an attempt to depict the visual manifestation of brain-wave activity, and his views were complemented by the work of his artist associate Brion Gysin who attempted in his paintings to actively *produce* these neurological effects. This wasn't so improbable as it may at first sound. In 1984, a group of British researchers found that some people found a certain pattern of stripes painful to look at. Some subjects reported headaches and others, particularly those predisposed to the conditions, suffered migraines and epileptic fits when shown a pattern resembling a circle filled with alternating black and white vertical stripes of a specific frequency.

Given that a simple pattern is capable of producing such profound symptoms, it may well be suggested that a more sophisticated pattern would be able to trigger more specific neurological events. We may consider the type of pattern that would be required to trigger spontaneous orgasm in particular. And whether this could be super-charged or fine-tuned to result in some kind ecstasy-death.

Further to this, we may conceive an anti-theft device the size and shape of a credit-card, but printed with the pattern to be carried in the wallet and never removed, except by muggers and pickpockets, who would ejaculate themselves comatose in the course of examining their booty. It could well be the pattern would turn out to be abstract, or something like a heraldic device, or even a word. Gysin himself has speculated that the origin of language in early humans may have been due to exposure to flicker.

The train picked up speed and we hurtled through the ghostly stations of remote outback towns. I was increasingly struck by the alternating familiarity and strangeness of the place-names. As we crossed into South Australia from New South Wales the towns we sped through less frequently bore names transplanted from Britain, but more usually came anglicisations of Aboriginal words: Yunta, Wirraminna, Kingoonya, Tarcoola, Coonana. From where I sat, the transition was from plagiarism to nonsense. My state of mind, engendered by flicker, fatigue and countless shifts of time zone, made the unfamiliar configurations of letters appear more like pictograms than words. And as the hours passed, filled with nothing but booze and crafty spliffs, the words vanished altogether. For all I knew, I could have been on the other side of the world.

As the hours passed the light outside became less than the inside, and the glass turned from a window to a mirror, the outside gradually morphed into the inside. And for all I knew, I could have been on the other side of the glass.

N THE CABIN I was worried the Conductor would smell the pot-smoke and throw me off so I opened the window onto the Southern Hemisphere. Only now did it strike me that I had forfeited my stellar heritage when I left Blighty[*], for gone were the familiar constellations of the Northern Hemisphere that had shone overhead for the whole duration of my life, unceasing in their movement as they were constant in their presence. Andromeda—lost forever (more or less)! And all the constellations of the Southern Hemisphere[†] were vivid now, away

---

[*] The word "Blighty" meaning home, and more generally England, derived in the early 20th century from the Urdu word *bilayati*, meaning foreign. Thus we have a word whose meaning in English is its own direct compliment in its original language, thus presenting unparalleled problems for translators.

[†] Edmund Halley had mapped these southern constellations from southern Africa in 1679, but Abbé Nicolas Louis de Lacaille had made surveys in 1752 and 1763, naming fourteen "new" constellations from the instrumentation and technology of his time. Sir William Herschel and his son Sir John Herschel had conducted a further survey in 1864.

Long before this, the stars had been mapped by the native Australians, probably even before the ancient Greeks, who

from the pollution of the city, but in their place I could locate only the Southern Cross.

started mapping their section of sky in about the fourth century BC, naming a different set of constellations from the Romans who started later. All of these systems posited different ways of reading the same symbols.

The Southern Cross was officially identified, as Crux Australis, by the French Astronomer Augustin Royer in 1679. It comprises of five stars: Alpha Crucis, Beta, Crucis, Delta Crucis and Epsilon Crucis, and is to be found in the southern celestial hemisphere about a third of the way between the South Pole and the equator.

Given its relatively recent discovery by Europeans, the closest thing to a traditional stellar legend is to be found in the "Purgatorio" section of the *Divine Comedy*, wherein Danté assigns the moral virtues of justice, prudence, temperance and fortitude to the constellation's four main stars.

The Southern Cross is not generally visible in the Northern Hemisphere, and is widely regarded as representative of Australia, since it marks the topographical location on the planet. It is the most prominent of the two features that distinguish the Australian national flag from the British Blue Ensign, the other being the seven-pointed Commonwealth Star.

GIRL IN A SUMMER DRESS presents the curved nape of her neck, her head is bent forward at such an angle as to present a cleavage between her shoulder blades equivalent to the one between her breasts. This position forms a plane on the triangle of flesh bounded by the apex of her left shoulder blade, the left hinge of her jawbone and a point approximately three inches directly above the nipple of her left breast which is revealed in its entirety, her dress having ridden well down.

This triangle is bisected by a necklace of ostensible pearls that circles from below her chin into her blondish hair, the mass of which has been thrown back by the violence of the angle of her head, plainly exposing the entire orifice of her left ear. A less violent but prolonged movement has caused the fastener of the necklace to slip around her neck to a position just above her oesophagus. Above the necklace, the girl's chin juts out, her mouth open as wide as it could comfortably be held for a prolonged period. Her lips are tinted a conventional red and between them her tongue protrudes two inches to make contact with the tip of an erect penis. She is licking the top of the helmet and its slit makes tentative contact with the middle point of her bottom lip, a generous residue of lipstick can be observed where it has rubbed on the bottom of the glans. The shaft of the penis is grasped in the girl's left hand, the wrist of which is resting below her left breast and agitating the nipple which has assumed a shape which may be expressed as a sine wave compressed along the $x$-axis.

Below her forearm the material of a dress is visible, it is impossible to discern any feature of its cut since it has ridden up and now covers an area only about fifteen centimetres high, centred on the girl's navel. It is plainly a lightweight summer dress made of cotton and printed in alternating blue and white stripes approximately one inch in width; the girl is completely exposed below this. Although her buttocks are hidden from view by her position, the right one bears her weight and behind it appears a multi-coloured floral background; maybe a sheet or blanket, but given the intensity of the design an coverless mattress seems more likely.

The back of the girl's left thigh is catching the light and the flesh appears slightly darker towards the front. Her legs are forty degrees apart and her pubis is entirely visible, its generous hair is a deep russet in hue. Even though the area between her legs is underlit it is possible to distinguish the labia, which are dark and of moderate length, and even the opening to her vagina may be vaguely discerned.

Between the girl's legs, resting across her right thigh halfway up, there protrudes the knee of a second girl's right leg, it is contained within an almost opaque white stocking. From the knee downward the leg is held tightly against the inside of the first's left thigh. Both of their legs are resting on the left leg of a third girl, which is held apart from her right at an angle of sixty degrees. High up on the left thigh rests the right hand of the second girl, the blatantly false nails of its four fingers are polished with a garish red varnish which appears to sparkle in the light. The thumb nail is similarly adorned but cannot be seen clearly as it faces the other way, digging into the outside of her own thigh near the top of her stocking.

The anterior part of the third girl's vagina is clearly visible, she has apparently been shaved recently but a thin layer of fuzz has started to re-cover the area. Her labia are quite long and no darker than the skin which surrounds them. They are splayed wide apart, presumably by the second girl's hand since she is well lubricated and the area between her left thigh and the hand of second girl glistens with liberal secretions. The inside of her vagina appears quite red, perhaps inflamed by the second girl's nails.

Both of the third girl's buttocks rest on a pale-lilac sheet, apparently satin, which passes beneath her right buttock to reappear around the top of the thigh. Her back is slightly arched and her right leg is held out, bent sharply at the knee, to provide uninhibited access to her vagina.

The sheet continues around her belly, between her navel and the base of her breasts, before passing out of sight beneath the right arm of the second girl. On the way it is partially obscured by the right arm of the third girl just below a horizontal cut which is about three inches long, obviously recent, and although it appears quite deep, it is not bleeding. This cut points directly in-line toward the nipple of her right breast, itself a deep shade of rose fading into a lighter aureole, it is in the process of becoming erect. Her breasts are large, and from this angle point upward to form almost perfect hemispheres, though the right one is slightly crushed at its outer extremity by her upper arm as she reaches over towards the other two girls.

The neck of the third girl is hidden by the second girl's unusually large hand as she pulls her toward her closer, simultaneously caressing her ash blonde hair. The third girl's face is turned toward the second so that her gold-ringed right ear is the only visible facial feature except for half an inch of tongue which is extended into the mouth of the second girl whose head is turned sharply to the right to meet her, thus exposing the length of her throat which is bisected halfway down by a necklace of red and white beads.

The second girl's tongue protrudes through her half open mouth, her lips are painted a complimentary tone to her nails and her brilliant white teeth threaten to bite down on her co-osculator. Her eyes are tightly closed, the lids screwed up together beneath the long fringe of her copper-hued hair, which entangles with the other girl's ash-blonde. Her position appears extremely uncomfortable, but her beatific expression and the fact that the nipples of her small breasts are fully erected belie this. This erection may be assumed to have been effected by the friction of the hair the first girl in the case of the left, or the fingers of the third girl in the case of the right. This hand, with nails painted a red slightly duller than those of the second girl and bearing a wide wedding band, now entwined in the hair of the first girl and moving toward the lilac satin suspender-belt of the second girl. Beneath this belt the hand of the first girl obscures the crotch of the second girl in such a way as to make it impossible to tell whether the penis which she is so enthusiastically sucking is actually a double ended dildo inserted in her vagina, or an actual penis which would entail the second girl being a trans-sexual.

There is a small rectangle missing from each corner of the tableau, and in each of these a figure "7" may be observed, together with the symbol "♠'.

HE REVERSE OF THE CARD is pale grey, with vertical stripes that are hardly darker; between the darker stripes, in the middle of the lighter bands, rises a line of small designs, all identical, in a very dark grey: a floret, a kind of cross: an elongated main shape, like a table knife but wider, coming to a point at one end and slightly swollen at the other, cut across by a much shorter cross-piece consisting of two flame-shaped projections laid out symmetrically on either side of the main axis, just at the base of the swollen part, that is to say at about a third of the total length.

 HADN'T THE FOGGIEST IDEA how this card had got into my jacket pocket and now it assumed a divinatory significance`, and

It has been observed that the photographs on nudie decks lend them more of a resemblance to the pictorial cards of the Tarot than to the abstract symbols of a traditional deck. In a traditional deck each suit corresponds to a suit of the minor arcana of the Tarot: Clubs to Wands, Diamonds to Pentacles, Hearts to Cups and Spades to Swords. In Aleister Crowley's *Tarot Divination:*

Card XLI

The Lord of Unstable Effort

*Seven of Swords*

Two Angelic Radiating Hands as before, each holding three swords. A third hand holds up a single sword in the centre. The points of all the swords *just touch* each other, the central sword not altogether dividing them.

The Rose of the previous symbols of this suit is held up by the same hand which holds the central sword: as if the victory were at its disposal. Symbols of ☽ and ♒.

Partial success. Yielding when victory is within grasp, as if the last reserves of strength were used up. Inclination to lose when on the point of gaining, through not continuing the effort. Love of abundance, fascinated by display, given to compliments, affronts and insolences, and to spy upon others. Inclined to

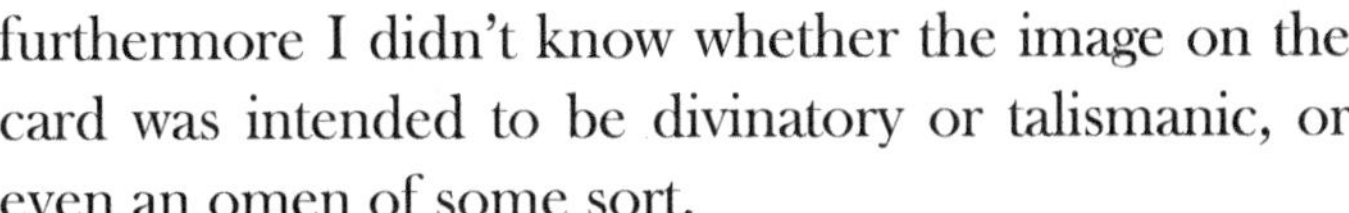

furthermore I didn't know whether the image on the card was intended to be divinatory or talismanic, or even an omen of some sort.

---

betray confidences, not always intentionally. Rather vacillatory and unreliable.

It should be observed that Crowley's descriptions are notoriously tainted by his misogyny and that the sevens, being Venusian cards, proffer particularly questionable interpretations.

# II

# THE PINK
# AND THE GREY

Dans le sacrifice, la victime était choisie de telle
manière que sa perfection achevat de render
sensible la brutalité de la mort.

*— Georges Bataille*

Sur sa poitrine à la peau blanche de dessins
Compliqués sont formés d'un côté par des veines;
Son corset par devant a ses agrafes pleines
De reflets sur leur cuivre étincelant, plat.....

*— Raymond Roussel*

LOSE IN THE BLACKNESS there was an enormous flash of lightning and the thunder came less than a second later. It shook the hired Land Rover and I clutched at the steering wheel, nails biting into my palms. There had been fog all the way from the town then it had changed to misty rain and now it poured in millions of heavy drops and they beat a crushing rhythmic tattoo on the roof and bonnet.

I slowed down to train my torch on the map. I was precisely one mile beyond the beginning of the high stone wall with the broken glass bottles embedded in the top, but I couldn't see a thing. Then, as though in answer to my need, the downpour slackened for a moment and another flash of lightning provided me with the required light.

The wire was at least twelve feet high and for a split second I could see the embedded razors flash like jewels. I shuddered and clutched again at the wheel as I saw the opening close ahead.

I turned slowly, straining my eyes through the quickening rain to the enormous gate as it ground open over the wet ground. For a second I thought I saw an old man behind it, waving me in with a friendly nod. I shuddered again and knew it had to be an illusion. There could be no one out on a night like this.

The dirt road began to ascend, the water-filled ruts were rushing streams and I had to shift to the lowest gear to keep traction. Then, just as the map indicated, looming ahead like a shadowy spectre in the black night, was the old ghost town.

At this point the road skirted the edge of a pre-cipitous cliff that leaped down a hundred feet to jagged boulders and I kept my attention riveted on the unprotected edge. When the road turned inward I looked up. Another close flash seemed to crackle the air and illuminate the old settlement. Even through the heavy rain I could make out the dilapi-dated wooden buildings, the battered old water tower. A second zigzag of lightning cut across the stables and into the cemetery, gouging a deep furrow and rendered the stones almost readable. Close by a dingo cackled.

"A cackling dingo?" I rolled down the side window got a bucket of water in the face for my trouble

I pulled up in front of the American Hotel and parked up. I grabbed my suitcase and rushed under the veranda, put down my bag and lifted the heavy knocker with both hands, straining to get it out all the way, and let it go. The impressive door vibrated with the blow and I could hear the echo of the sound bouncing through the halls and then the boom was reinforced somewhere, changed slightly in pitch, and funnelled back down to the front door in another bone-shattering blow.

There was a rumble of heavy iron bolts being moved, the lifting of mighty catches, and the door began to move. It creaked and halted. A flash of light made diamonds of the dancing raindrops. I pushed from the outside until there was enough room for me to squeeze through. My way was barred by a beautiful woman.

"You must be the new recruit," she said, with some kind of exotic accent I didn't recognise.

"That's about the size of it. Did the Director arrive as planned?"

"He's in bed, like everyone else. I'm his uh daughter. Do come in."

Despite the offer she made no attempt to move and my dampened topcoat pressed against her flimsy silken dressing gown as I squeezed through the narrow opening. As we stepped into the light inside I saw that she was a dead spit for Brigitte Bardot c. MCMLV.

The rain had glued the sheer material to her curvaceous body and rendered the white silk translucent. I could see very well that she was naked beneath the thin garment. The points of her nipples were clearly defined as they strained from her jutting breasts, the flatness of her belly was interrupted by a pert navel, beneath which the fleecy isosceles seemed to beckon.

Strangely, although she appeared to be dressed for bed, her heels were higher than my cock, but we would soon be rectifying that.

"You've got me all wet." she went, double-entendrely.

Taking up a candelabra, she led the way through the deserted old colonial hotel, past wooden panelling hung with erotic prints, the harvest of centuries. Up a winding staircase to my extravagantly furnished room, with a welcoming fire blazing in the hearth. I noticed a bookcase by the head of the bed, it was filled with uniformly bound volumes of the classics of erotica.

I stood with my back to the blazing fire, warming my arse and admiring my gracious hostess as she fixed me a scotch and American from the mini-bar. It wasn't my customary tipple but I wasn't about to complain, that would call attention to the inadequacies of their intelligence. As she handed me the glass she pressed her lips to mine in an impromptu, though languid kiss. The vibration of the long drive had given me Satan's own hard-on and this was the last straw, my cock ballooned up to its full extent like a driver's side airbag going off, except it didn't deflate within micro-seconds. The unembarrassed woman pressed herself against me and tested the erection against her, I felt one of her hands move downward to explore.

"Ohhh," she went, crestfallen, "and I have to keep myself pure... I have to work in the morning. It's the rules and if daddy found out, he'd... but maybe if you promise not to touch me... I could just..."

By way of explanation, she unzipped my fly and my penis burst out like a perverse jack-in-the-box..

"I'm sorry, but this is really all I can do... for now. Even doing this would get me into so much trouble if anyone found out."

Her fingers fluttered round the swollen organ as nimble as hummingbirds. One tickled beneath the tight sac of my scrotum while the other pulled the foreskin up and down over the helmet until the lubricant flowed and she used the fluid to ease her fingers up and down the seam of the helmet. After a couple of minutes of that I could contain myself no longer and exploded a thick bolt of semen which traversed the space between us and deposited itself on the fabric over her left breast just below the nipple. The balance of my testicles didn't possess the energy to project itself so far and it slipped through her fingers onto the thick russet carpet.

"So that was your debut offload for us. But, you must be exhausted. Daddy will tell you everything you need to know tomorrow."

As she left she put her fingers to the sticky patch on her left breast, already starting to dry in the glow of the fire, then she giggled emphatically.

AWOKE THE NEXT MORNING refreshed and ready for action. I made my toilet— just in time. It was an unsettling shade of cerise porcelain with a rosewood seat. While I was sitting on it the Director called up and invited me to join him for breakfast. The phone was a space-age hands-free job, and fortunately the video-link was wired to a detector in the toilet-seat, which defaulted the channel to audio only. The Director instructed the integrated printer to produce a map indicating the route to the dining room, which was useful, and also a copy of the organisation's official newsletter.

*The Organ* informed me that the organisation, so secret that it was officially nameless, was usually referred to internally as "The Org". The precise origin of the epithet was unknown, but it might have derived from *orgy* without the "y", as in "why?", or from *orgone* without the "one", i.e. "1". Fascinating stuff.

I arrived promptly and ordered some boiled eggs with Vegemite soldiers whilst the Director indulged in a steak with a fried egg on it, but he talked more than he ate.

"The arms of our noble organisation..." he went, gesturing at the crest hanging over the impressive fireplace: rose, a saltire ash-grey, charged with a grenade invers argent. The motto: 'ΜΑΝΕ ΘΕΣΕΛ ΨΑΡΗΣ'.

Mane Thecal Phares, meaning 'counted weighed divided', the words emblazoned in blood on the wall at Balshazzar's feast (Daniel 5:XXV), or was it fire?"

"Hmmm..."

"We operate a number of departments and research into physical, physiological and psychological aspects of the sexual act and also its influence in culture-space, that is to say the representation of sexual phenomena in image, word and sound. Before we assign you to a department you should get an overview of their respective roles. This morning there's an interesting experiment in multiplicity in lab 23b that you could usefully observe. I'll take you down there myself. Then you can get some lunch in the mess, and maybe make time for a chat with #579 about his particular project. This evening there's going to be a bit of a bash to celebrate his project's provisional completion and you might as well know what you're getting pissed for."

Y FIRST ASSIGNMENT was to monitor an experiment in multiplicity. The purpose of the experiment was to ascertain the point when the quantity of sex produced a qualitative change in the subject's brain waves. Having determined the kind of electrical rhythms which were generated in the brain by stimulating different erogenous zones, we were now going to record the interference patterns which arose from simultaneous stimulation of combinations of zones. The experiment had to be of a prolonged duration in order to obtain reliable readings.

The set-up was pretty sophisticated with the observation chamber done up like an upmarket motel room, or maybe it was supposed to just look homely but came over unconvincing for the same reasons motel rooms did. The Director and I watched from the control-booth, divided from the main chamber by a wall of glass. The window could be polarised into a one-way mirror by the flick of a switch on the impressive console beneath it, but we were all professionals here and it had already been determined that the act of being observed observing did not skew the data significantly in this particular experiment. I was informed that the attendants would signified on the console monitor by subscripted lower case Greek characters, thus $\alpha$, $\beta$, $\chi$, $\delta$, and the subject by $\mathbf{x}$[*]

---



[*] Despite its low frequency of occurrence and its high degree of redundancy, the letter X has more technical and social uses than any other letter in the English alphabet.

As well as an unknown or unspecified person or thing, e.g. "Mr X", or conversely it may indicate a specific position, as in "X marks the spot".

In algebra, a lower case letter X is used (usually italicized) to signify the first unknown quantity and in geometry to signify the first co-ordinate. In arithmetic it represents multiplication, the only letter that functions as a sign for one of the four basic operators, usually replaced by an asterisk (*) in computing contexts to avoid ambiguity.

In Boolean logic, it can stand for "don't know" or "don't care" in lieu of true (1) or false (0).

To the Romans X signified the number ten and as such it represents the differences between a number-set that includes a zero and one that doesn't. The Roman numeral X (for 10) is used in modulus-11 check digits, such as the one that concludes an ISBN (International Standard Book Number), to force-fit the number 10 into one character space.

Outside of mathematics, this letter may symbolize incorrectness, a kiss or a vote, or be used as a signature by a person unable to write their name.

The X in "Xmas" stands not for the sign of the cross but for the initial of Christ's surname in the Greek alphabet. It may symbolize a capture in Chess (e.g. QxP), a draw on UK football pool coupons, a sexual hybrid in horticulture, a male in genetics (the X chromosome), or magnification in photography (10x).

"We do everything possible to make the subject comfortable. In this case electrodes cannot be inserted into the orifices since these are needed for... uh... other purposes. So there are electrodes concealed in the mattress, these are ultra-sensitive radio-receivers capable of picking up the faintest signals from deep within the brain. They're tuned to lock into and track specific brain-waves. Unfortunately gross-motor activity causes electronic noise, which then impacts on signal strength, so we have to secure the subject, this doesn't taint the data since we're careful to screen subjects to include those with a receptivity to restraint."

As we watched a α led x into the room, she was clad in a velvet robe, the collar trimmed with fur, and

---

The X certificate for films was introduced in England in 1951 to signify films unsuitable for children (one of the first was *The Quatermass Xperiment*) and endured until 1982 when it was superseded by the more obvious but less evocative 18 and R18 classifications. The pornographic motion-picture industry differentiates between "soft X" films which include nudity and simulated sex-scenes, and "hard X" (or XXX) films which include unsimulated sex-scenes usually featuring prominent erections and ejaculations. XXX is also used to signify hard liquor, sometimes bootlegged.

X is the twenty-fourth letter of the Roman alphabet, and this number has special significance as the number of hours in a day, and as the number of combinations of four things, i.e. $4!=4\times3\times2\times1=24$.

she bore an uncanny resemblance to the director's daughter.

"Errr, uncanny, yes... Actually it is my daughter. She's... uh... done her hair differently." explained the Director when I drew this to his attention.

"You don't have any qualms about her entering this line of work?"

"None whatsoever!" replied the Director indignantly, "it would be hypocritical otherwise. I wouldn't ask someone else's daughter to do anything I wouldn't ask of my own."

"Of course not, I intended no offence."

"Think nothing of it."

"Alpha attendant, please engage as specified..." announced a synthetic voice. $\alpha$ said something and $x$ giggled soundlessly.

"Whoops!" went the Director, throwing a switch. Immediately her girlish laughter filled our chamber in hi-fidelity quadraphonic sound.

The attendant graciously removed the girl's robe and hung it on a convenient hook, beneath it she was as naked as the previous evening. Under the unforgiving fluorescent light I observed that her body was clinically flawless, so there was nothing to forgive. She lay down on the bed and allowed him to fasten her wrists and ankles to each of the four bedknobs with a thick golden cord.

"That cord *is* actually 24ct gold," the Director elaborated, "it's highly conductive, and by changes in its resistance we can compensate for the small degree of movement it allows."

The naked girl now lay spread-eagled on the bed with her sex exposed toward us at a jaunty angle, and α was endeavouring to shed his uniform as fast as possible.

"Well, I'll leave you to it." went the Director, taking his leave.

The eager attendant was teasing the girl by trailing his rapidly erectifying penis over her face, she lunged and snapped playfully at it but wasn't able to secure a hold until it was thoroughly engorged, and even then he allowed her to take just the tip of it, which she accepted with a rapt expression. As she squirmed on the bed, my monitor began to pop-up dialog boxes and drop-down menus as various interrupts were received and processed.

The demarcation of the helmet of α's penis from its shaft granted a striking testament to the pride which he took in his work. As its volume increased he fed more of its length into x's hungry mouth and she sucked enthusiastically in wordless answer.

"Beta attendant, please engage as specified..." the tannoy now announced, and with no further prompting a second attendant appeared through the door.

The first attendant (α) noted his arrival and withdrew from her mouth, a resounding pop testified to her reluctance to part with the organ for even a moment, but the opening thus created was soon filled by the new arrival, who assumed the required degree of atrophy even faster than his predecessor, who had moved around and was now stimulating x's right breast with his organ, he drew around it, spiralling in on the nipple leaving a pattern in saliva and lubricant on its surface.

Meanwhile β was enjoying his role equally as much as his predecessor. He moved around so that his knees were either side of her head, and his penis could gain entry to the very depths of her throat. x was evidently aroused, her hips ground out an unanswered rhythm further down the bed, and I gathered it would be pretty moist in there.

"Gamma attendant, please engage as specified..." went the voice again, the response was even more eager and the game of musical erogenous zones continued with β taking up a position on her left side and α moving down to her crotch. χ's first action was to lower himself onto the girl's face, he fetished his penis in her hair as she avidly licked at his thus presented perineum. At the very instant her tongue probed into the folds of his anus, α suddenly thrust his swollen organ into her cunt. Her lubrications produced an audible squelch as they were suddenly displaced by the intruder, and her vocal reaction was no less earnest when she managed to momentarily divert herself from the rim job at hand. All this time, β was amusing himself with the task of erecting her left nipple to its zenith using only his testicles, and succeeding.

α continued to pump rhythmically into x's cunt and her hindquarters rose up to meet him at each thrust, as best they could within her bonds. At last he could contain him self no longer, with an inhuman grunt he extracted his penis and squirted in a copious gush over the writhing girl's mons venus and the inside of her thighs. Meanwhile β had meanwhile diverted his attentions to her right breast, leaving a vacancy for α to move up and wipe himself on the left, tickling the nipple with his slimy tip still exuding over it.

"Delta attendant, please engage as specified..." went the relentless speaker, though no fourth attendant appeared.

χ's rim job apparently met with approval, his penis had assumed frightening aspect and his intentions rendered it even more so as he took up his new position between her thighs. Lifting and parting her buttocks for easier access, he was to pleasure her in a similar way but a different manner. Her anus, thus exposed, was a perfect little pink-brown thing, and looked much too modest for so terrifying an instrument, but utilising the discharge of his predecessor as lubrication, χ worked the tip of his prick into the breach until a hold was secured. The muscles of x's buttocks contracted in waves as they received conflicting messages from the pain and pleasure centres of her brain.

"Delta attendant, please engage as specified. This is your second call..." went the speaker again, there was still no sign of him.

It was probably to $\delta$'s advantage that he was late, for the patience of $\beta$, currently still installed at her left breast, was now repaid as a thick jet of semen shot in an arc over the dome to spatter onto x's left-turned face. As she moved her head, the stream ran over her lips and down her cheek to disappear into her copious coiffure, a little of it collecting in the shell of her ear. Her tongue flicked desperately around her lips to taste as much of the precious load as possible.

Belatedly, $\delta$ now appeared, breathless and already in a state of arousal. He wasted no time and rudely introduced his penis into x's cum-stained mouth. She was obviously fatigued by now, and had to take frequent breaks in her suckling in order to take deep breaths, but as $\alpha$ and $\beta$ continued to stimulate her nipples and $\chi$'s anal ministrations reached fever pitch, terminating the session was obviously the furthest thing from her mind.

At this point $\chi$ took advantage of the vacancy in her cunt to introduce his thumb to the opening, and the effect was instantaneous. With every major orifice filled, her orgasm was inevitable and, when it came, it was terrifying in its intensity. Her laboured breathing filled the control room, the point at which the heavy breaths became moans was indiscernible, as was the point when the moans became screams. The movement of her hindquarters, previously fluid, now became violent and seemingly spiteful as she battered $\chi$'s organ with her rump, to his immense satisfaction even though he was forced to withdraw his anterior digit and grab a hold of each of her thighs in a bid to keep his position. $\delta$, meanwhile, continued to worry the girl's mouth as she struggled to draw breath. There was to be no respite from the attendants' attentions as $\times$ twisted beneath them, they had been instructed to continue until relieved, and now $\alpha$ and $\beta$, still stationed at each breast, were starting to re-harden at the sight of $\times$'s tangible pleasure. Suddenly $\chi$'s face contorted into a mask of excruciating relief as he flooded her bowels with his issue. This seemed to extinguish some of the fire in the girl's loins, and her motions became languid once more, her expec-torations turning to little sobs of pleasure. As he withdrew, she expelled a small quantity of the genetic tribute, streaked with a little of her blood, from her irritated anus as if to certify to the authenticity of $\chi$'s joy. The little puckered ring had assumed a purple tinge of bruising, as if it were glowing with orgones.

The girl was cyborgasmically bankrupt, but still she had to minister to the needs of the last-comer. With an air of worldly resignation she suckled $\delta$'s penis, occasionally twitching or sobbing as a straggling current of orgasm washed over her, much to his arousal. His penis was now assuming the final stages of extrusion that immediately preceded explosion. Frustrated with x's previous scant attentions, δ now plunged his member earnestly into the depth's of x's throat and soon enough the copious semen over-flowed from her lips and down her chin and neck.

"All attendants: disengage forthwith." went the voice, presently.

α and β looked crestfallen at this announcement, both their organs were ready for more action. Urgently they got in a last good breast-frotch and came in virtual unison, flooding x's upper torso with milky dew which dribbled over their surface to collect in the valley between her breasts. x appeared somewhat ambivalent at this unexpected bonus.

"All attendants. Disengage immediately," the voice announced in the same monotone, adding ominously, "you are reminded of the sanctions corresponding with non-compliance with authorised directives."

The attendants exchanged a high-five and departed swiftly, δ pausing to release each of her golden bonds. x's wrists and ankles were slightly chaffed by the ropes and there was an obvious stiffness in her joints, but on the whole she appeared none the worse for her afternoon's work, and she would be amply compensated. Leaving her to rest, I threw the switch that rendered the window opaque and nipped off to get a cup of tea from the vending machine.

When I got back, she was dead.

COULDN'T FIGURE OUT what the problem was, there were no marks on her, but there was no pulse either and she was already stone cold, which seemed odd given she couldn't have been dead for more than the five minutes of my absence.

Obviously this wasn't a happy development for my first morning's work, and I wasn't sure about what would be the best way of breaking the news to my boss, the Director, who just happened to be her father. I drank my polystyrene-cup of tea while I chewed it over, and found that I had inadvertently eaten an entire packet of Tim-Tams while I'd been deliberating. It seemed pointless procrastinating further so I picked up the receiver and dialled 23 for a direct line to the Director.

"Hello." he went.

"I'm terribly sorry, Herr Director, but your daughter appears to have been fucked to death. It really wasn't my fault." I went.

"Eh? What," he went, then "Oh I see! Aghh! Wait! I'll be right there!" He seemed upset, but that was understandable.

A couple of minutes later he burst into the control booth. Immediately I noticed that he was brandishing a huge samurai sword over his head.

"Murderer!" he bellowed, and the word echoed round the lab, "Murdererurdererrdererdererererrer-err!" and I felt the sword swish a swathe through the air just by my right ear.

"She's fucking dead!" the old man gibbered, "Fucked! Fucked to all fuck! Fucked by too much fucking fucking! And you! You fucking *fucking* fucker! F-f-f-f-shit!"

He'd gone west with a vengeance, now he charged me with the huge scary blade outstretched to kebabulate me.

"Oh bugger!" I went, then without thinking I planted my right winklepicker square in the old cunt's bollocks, he grunted, pulled a face and then fell to his knees, gibbering with agony.

"Sorry about that, you sad old fuck! But you asked for it." I went sympathetically.

The poor sod appeared to have lost his marbles for good, he was rolling around the floor clutching his injured crotch and cackling maniacally. Eventually he brought himself to speak, stammering in a voice that was breaking with emotion. "Your face! I had you going! You daft cunt!"

He painfully picked himself up and dusted himself off, went to a cupboard and took out a pair of surgical gloves,  then went into the room and over to the bed where his defunct offspring was laid. Parting the labia major and minor with his left hand, he reached his right into her cunt momentarily. Within a couple of seconds of seconds the girl stirred, murmured and then her eyes flicked open. She was apparently none the worse for her experience and sat patiently awaiting her debriefing. The Director came back into the control booth.

"A symbol-hierarchy integrity threshold event." he elucidated and wiped a tear from his eye, then good-naturedly slapped me on the back. "Gets 'em every time! A true laugh riot, I never get tired of it! A quick poke of the reset button and she's right as rain."

"A cyborg? And here was me shitting a brick!"

"Yes... and no. Our girls are all 100% flesh and blood, well 96.235%. The shells are actually con-structed in clone-tanks, then adjusted with injections of nanotechnological agents. We replace some of the brain functions with electronics to make them compatible with our computer network. Our biggest problem was figuring out what to call them, we settled on 'Models', but during development we referred to the first as Fuck Object (eXperimental) Mk. 1, abbreviated to FOX, and that name stuck. I think of them all as my daughters."

"But if they don't have human brains, what's to be learned by analysing their brain-waves?"

"What are you? Some kind of organocentric wise guy?"

"Err... And they're all cloned from the same stock..."

"...which explains the consistency between the different models as you earlier observed."

"So did you get the DNA from BB herself? Does that explain the resemblance?"

"No."

"No you didn't or no it doesn't?"

"Just no. You probably aren't aware of the thriving black market in bootleg DNA. Unethical biologists are striving for a conjectured wealth or fame gene, and blood samples of the rich and famous routinely go astray following hospital visits. Well, routinely may be putting it a bit strong, but it's a common enough crime that it has its own name, they call it kiDNApping. Somewhat ironically, the price of bootleg DNA is so astronomical that only the super-wealthy themselves can afford it."

"Hmm... Stranger things have happened, and will. Do your attendants have any qualms about inter-course with non-human organisms?"

"Wouldn't you?" the Director went, gesturing toward the eminently shagworthy erotomaton.

"Probably not..."

"Indeed..."

"Yeah yeah... I know all about that stuff. As soon as you come up with a decent test for an intelligent

---

The best-known benchmark of "machine" "intelligence" was posited by the British mathematician Alan Turing in what is now referred to as the Turing test, intended as a test of whether a machine can reasonably be said to think or not.

According to this experiment, the computer which is claimed to think and a human volunteer are both hidden from the view of a perceptive interrogator who has to try and decide which of the two is the computer and which is the human being merely by putting probing questions to each of them. Thus:

> Q: Please write a limerick on a Classical topic.
> A: Count me out on this one. I never could write poetry.
> Q: OK, we're playing chess, I have my Q at my Q1 and my K at K1, and no other pieces. You have only K at K6 and R at R1. What's your move?
> A: (After a pause of 15 seconds) R-R8 mate.

These questions, and the answers thereto, are transmitted in an impersonal fashion, by teletype for instance. The interrogator is not allowed any information about either of the other parties except that which is obtained merely from this Q&A session. The human subject should seek to persuade the interrogator that they are indeed the human being and that the other subject is the computer, but the computer can be programmed to "lie" so as to try to convince the interrogator that it is actually the human. If the interrogator is unable to identify the real human subject in any consistent way, then the computer or the computer's program, or programmer, or designer, or whoever or whatever, is deemed to have passed the test.

It may be argued that this test is actually weighted against the computer. If the roles were reversed, with the human machine the humanist cunts move the goalposts and refuse to recognise the benchmark as significant. Fuck that Chinese Room* shit! I fucking invented Strong AI!"

---

posing as a computer and the computer answering truthfully, then it would be only too easy for the interrogator to find out which was which. They would merely have to ask the subject to perform some very complicated calculation. A computer would be able to answer accurately and immediately but the most proficient human would be slower and not as reliable.

* The Chinese Room (or Chinese Box) thought experiment was proposed by the American philosopher J.R. Searle in a 1980 paper. The experiment supposes that a subject, fluent in English but with no knowledge of Chinese, is locked in a room with a batch of writing in Chinese, together with instructions, in English, for returning particular batches of Chinese (i.e. "answers") by way of response to incoming batches ("questions"). This is done by manipulating uninterrupted batches of Chinese script recognized purely by its shape. The experiment is supposed to undermine the case for Strong AI by proving that the subject has everything that can be supplied by way of a program and yet possesses no understanding of Chinese.

The experiment has been heavily criticized, most convincingly on the grounds that it is the overall system that is more appropriately compared to a programmed computer rather than the central subject who merely shuffles the papers. Searle's responses to criticisms of his experiment insist that anything characterized as a thinker must have appropriate causal powers, and also that such powers essentially require a biology.

"Exactly! Whether they're religious or humanist, all these idiots who're so precious about their cold porridge! That's what your brain is, same colour, same texture, different taste though. So don't expect me to get all romantic about it. I've dissected more brains than you've had hot dinners and let me tell you..."

"Herr Director, forgive my interruption, but when it comes down to reductionism, I require no persuasion. I'm already a fundamentalist. I would gladly trade my non-existent immortal soul for, say, a tenner. That's my idea of a fucking sweet deal."

"Well, alright. But here's a case in point... I take it you're familiar with the Voigt-Kampff Altered Scale? It tests for empathy which androids supposedly can't mimic, or not quickly enough anyway. This is based on retinal dilation and blush-responses in reaction to shame-inducing questions."

"Uh-huh."

"Well, we tried it and discovered its biggest limitation was that most humans lack any significant empathic capacity either."

"Precisely. So we set about developing a foolproof test. We calculated that if you could invent a machine that could give the interrogator a really good fuck, then you could catch them off guard right afterwards..."

"...with their pants down!"

"Quite. And then they'd have to voluntarily endorse the machine as a living organism, or else we'd threaten to blackmail them into it."

"Well, Herr Director, I've got to hand it to you. That's the most utterly fucking brilliant plan I've ever heard of. Faaaaaaantastic!"

"Yes, in actual fact my mind is so terribly over-developed that I quite often experience an overwhelming urge to voluntarily reduce its effectiveness, often to the point of total collapse."

"I'm sure that a man of your intellect would require the most potent of consciousness restricting substances."

"Well, maybe you'd like to come and have a browse through my library, widely regarded as a veritable pharmatopia?"

"Maybe some other time... You know how it is, things to see, people to do... I'll take a brain-check though."

RETURNED TO THE HOTEL but there was no one at reception to give me my keys. I rang the brass bell on the counter to no avail. I could see the relevant bunch hanging on the key-board behind the desk but it seemed presumptuous to just take them. In the silence of the noon it seemed like everyone were taking a siesta, but if that was the case then surely the Director would have mentioned it.

I rang the bell again then lifted the counter-flap and went behind the desk. I knocked on the office door and tentatively poked my head through. And still not a soul. Now intrigued, I made my way through to the office and followed a mahogany-panelled corridor that led there-off. Detecting a faint hubbub sounded behind a door at the end, I approached, threw it open, and was met by a surprising sight. This room was set up like a communal dressing-room from a major West End theatre or something. There were two rows of twelve seats, arranged back to back before a long mirror and a smorgasbord of cosmetics. Each seat was occupied by a definition of pulchritude, and the seat at the end was occupied by the Director's daughter, who I'd just left on the slab in Lab 23b. And so was the seat next to her. And every single other seat but for a couple of absentees. The sitting girls were all dressed in Org reg robes, rose with ash-grey piping or vice-versa, and each of them was studiously removing their make-up, dabbing at their faces with oversize powder-puffs loaded with chemicals. Seeing them together like this it was obvious that their differentiations were expressed entirely in their choice of coiffures and cosmetics. I was perplexed and embarrassed in equal measure and would have made my apologies and departed forthwith but a FOX halfway down the left-hand row recognised me.

"Ladies! This is our newest recruit!" She went, getting up and pecking me formally, "now don't say you don't remember me!"

I was forced to assume that this was the FOX whose intimate acquaintance I had made on the previous evening. I went up and down the rows shaking hands and introducing myself and answering their polite questions.

"No, I haven't been formally assigned as yet."

"Around 9:00."

"Oh I see, around 9"."

"Absolutely!"

"Just a couple of days ago."

"Yes, that's right, a seaside resort on the south coast of the UK."

"Yes, it was terrible wasn't it? No, it was just before I left... that is to say *immediately* before. Haha..."

"Uh, no comment..."

Etc.

We seemed to be getting on like a house on fire, but the FOXes soon made their excuses and I was left alone with the erstwhile **x**.

"It was remiss of the Director not to mention it to you, but we're all getting ready for the big ball tonight... Still, I'm sure we can find a way to amuse ourselves. Come with me."

Intrigued, I followed her through a second door, and it led to a toilet cubicle adjacent to the communal shower. In the cool green tiled interior, she motioned me to sit upon the lowered seat and used some secret technique to dislodge the tile located at eye-level by my side. The gap thus exposed afforded an excellent view of the interior of the neighbouring shower-stalls. As the first FOX entered, I flinched as she stared straight into the gap.

"The missing bricks are hidden behind a one-way mirror on the other side." whispered my co-voyeur, "It's funny, the Director is so terribly fond of his one-way mirrors, yet it's not like we're bashful, is it?"

The veracity of each of these statements was confirmed by the voyee as she shed her robe. Standing with her back to the mirror, she spread her legs wide and touched the floor with one hand, peering behind herself to check the appearance of those parts which usually pass unobserved. Her anus unfolded slightly as she relaxed and probed a long-nailed finger inward to tease the puckered knot. Satisfied with her examination thus far, her fingers crossed the perineum, momentarily pausing to stroke there and test its sensitivity before moving forward to smooth down the pubic fleece and then separate the lips, the better to observe the inside of her treasury. Observing nothing untoward, she lingered there, stroking the fleshy folds all the way down to the tiny cerise button that grew as she did so. A drop of heavy dew form at the base of the lips and drizzled down to the button. Observing her face in the mirror her eyes stared straight into mine, and her slightly-parted mouth opened in a soundless gasp as she slipped her middle finger into herself.

Just then two more women entered, one cruelly twisted a control and the masturbating woman jolted upright as she was dowsed by the freezing shower. The newcomers laughed and the masturbator paused for a nervous moment before joining in, jokingly offering a finger for them to taste. They complied all too eagerly and in a moment the three were squirming over each other beneath the spouting jets, shedding their sodden robes, connecting fingers and tongues with mouths and genitals. More women entered the block and soon the floor seethed in a lottery of flesh. What wisps of clothing remained unshredded were rendered instantly translucent by the water as they rolled and splashed, squealing their delight and soaping each other with rare unguents.

This impromptu spectacle did not leave us observers unmoved. My co-voyeur swiftly removed her robe and stood before me splendid in her nakedness. Impatiently, she removed my trousers, removing them with difficulty for the preceding spectacle had engorged my penis to the same extent as it had moistened her cunt. This done, she threw herself into my lap, straddling me on the toilet-seat and sliding my manhood expertly into herself. There was nothing subtle about what happened next, there didn't have to be. She bobbed up and down like a lazy piston and my cock mushroomed inside her, filling her vagina so that displaced gleet squirted out under pressure each time she made a down stroke. Her breasts bounced majestically, and as they passed my mouth I snapped and fixed my eager lips to one and then the other, gently nibbling at the nipples which immediately displayed their approval. The poor girl didn't take long to approach her climax and within moments her eyes had misted and she bit her bottom lip in a fruitless bid to keep from crying out, which came as a choked moan which would have been heartbreaking under any other circumstance, as she collapsed into my arms. Heedless of ongoing moaning noises, which I chose to interpret as signals of pleasure, I continued to pump beneath her, thus prolonging her orgasm and the respective delicious contractions within her which in no time drew the fluids from me such that I thought the flood would never cease but till I was a hollow and dry, like a gourd, or something.

As the woman dismounted, she held a hand beneath her cunt and caught all of the semen as it drizzled out. I was touched to see that she did not waste this, but rather lapped it thirstily from her palm, wiping her still-sticky hands on her breasts when she had done so, the delicate tips which had barely begun to relax now stiffened again. I glanced back into the shower block and it was empty but for one girl, still the first for all I knew, she was sitting in the corner, still masturbating frenzidly, now softly sobbing to herself.

O #579 WAS a "reformed" hacker. He'd got his moniker from a telephone extension at a job he'd had years before where he'd put down some especially crafty shit. He'd been recruited by the Org and had an office in the old vicarage, there wasn't much equipment in here, just many shelves of pornographs and a mahogany desk under an impressive mess of paper. #579 sat in a leather armchair playing chess with himself. The pieces were gigantic, carved from rosewood and ebony. I looked closer and saw that the red pieces were in the form of the heroines of erotic literature: Juliette, Justine, Simon, Marcel, Helen, Carmecita, and the chateaus of Roissy and Gevaudin; the pawns were anonymous nymphs. The models for the black pieces were the giants of computing and cybernetics: Babbage, Lovelace (no relation?), Von Neuman, Turing, Shannon, Wiener, Bletchley Park and PARC.

---

The use of red as a substitute opposite for black in some chess sets is an exception to the general rule that red opposes black only when white is used as a field. In these cases "red vs. black" signifies a difference of the same order, and "white vs. red or black" signifies a difference of order.

"Ah, hello old chap," he went, "Glad you could make it. Do excuse the mess." he got up and shook my hand. I had a vague feeling of familiarity, as if we'd met before. He noticed me looking at his pieces.

"Ah – they didn't come like that, I swapped one side with one of the techies. You out to see his set. Looks damn weird. Ho hum... is that the time? Name your poison."

"You got any really cheap gnarly scotch?"

"Why yes! Co-op Special Blend, imported from the UK at great expense. I'm glad to meet a fellow aficionado."

"Yeah, expensive whisky tastes like cough medicine, or Cointreau. Fuck that!"

"Absolutely, when you drink whisky, you want it to taste like whisky...", he went over to a mini-bar in the corner and poured two generous tumblers and looked thoughtful, "Funny how you don't get free glasses with your petrol down here, uneconomical I guess."

"So what's the crack?"

"Well, I take it you're familiar with the Traveller's Companion Series*?"

---



* The first Traveller's Companion Series is often cited as the greatest achievement in the spectacular career of Maurice Girodias, unquestionably the most influential publisher of the twentieth century. Even an organ as conservative as the New

So what I have done is to scan the entire series into this machine. I had to scan them because I generally only have one hand free while I'm working, if you take my point. Then I analysed them, indexing the salient information about each scene, and used the resulting database to reassemble the scenes into a new novel."

At this juncture he handed me a small paperback, it bore the title *Rape vs. Murder.*

---

York Times acknowledged Girodias's Olympia Press as "a literary enterprise that has profoundly influenced contemporary writing and culture". Among the most prominent names that Girodias was the first to publish were Samuel Beckett, William Burroughs, Gregory Corso, J.P. Donleavy, Vladimir Nabokov, and he was to make available in English works by Georges Bataille, Nicolas Restif de la Bretonne, Jean Genet, Henry Miller, and the Marquis de Sade.

Based in Paris, he published roughly one hundred books in the distinctive olive-green wrappers of the first Traveller's Companion Series between 1955 and 1965. The imprint started off publishing high-quality mainstream erotica, but as it progressed Girodias indulged his taste for literary and experimental fiction, for a number of reasons, not all of them aesthetic.

Because he was publishing in English, the French censorship laws weren't a problem at first, and the books were brought back across the Channel or the Atlantic by servicemen and tourists. Eventually the authorities clamped down and there were later and less influential incarnations of the press (and the series) in London and New York, but the Paris operation remains crucial to the development of culture in the second half of this century.

"The title is derived from the second and penultimate books in the series..."

"Why not the first and last?"

"*The Enormous Sextet*? Not bad but not, I think, quite so good. Which reminds me, I must remember to use that title somewhere."

"How complex are the algorithms governing the book's construction?"

"The original inspiration for the experiment stemmed from a desire to see how the development of the series would reflect in the development of a narrative. I experimented with several types of juxtaposition, with varying degrees of randomness. I was inspired by the words of the Inspector in volume 76, 'Be just and if you can't be just be arbitrary.' By short-circuiting the usual associational connections I was able to produce a narrative which tells its story in its form rather than its content. The true story of the Traveller's Companion Series, that is."

"Does it actually make sense?"

"How much sense does any book make? It depends entirely on the reader... Some people never make it past Dr. Seuss, and some don't make it that far..."

"What about issues of intellectual ownership?"

"Well, what about them? We're talking about some of the biggest names in 20$^{th}$ century literature. After Girodias had published them (when nobody else would touch their stuff with a ten-foot pole) some of these ingrates became very hostile to him, so I don't think that clearances would be straightforward. What you see isn't a publication as such, it's a simple reorganisation of data presented as an internal discussion document, and still technically illegal at that."

"Yeah, these days culture is constrained more by notions of property than propriety. Cunts!"

"So, this party won't be a launch as such, since there can probably never be a publication. It tears me apart, I tell you! This has been my life's work! I drink to dull the pain, but it doesn't work... But it kinda alters it and that'll do for now. Now. More grog vicar?"

"Mmmm..."

We supped up and arranged meet at the do.

HE MESS HAD BEEN FESTOONED with balloons and streamers and a banner strung from the ceiling that said THANK FUCK THAT'S OVER WITH. I was too early. There were already clusters of blokes standing around clutching stubbies and a DJ was spinning classic strip-club cuts like stuff from the *Las Vegas Grind* compilations and virtually any Soft Cell track.

I couldn't see any sign of #579 and it was entirely likely that he was comatose already as was the custom since party was in his honour. I got a stubby and some bozo came over and started telling me an story of dubious authenticity about how he'd made his fortune selling patented "Reek-o-Semen" flavoured pre-formed potato snacks into gay nite-clubs, only to blow it when he diversified to cater for coprophages, their market already being saturated by mainstream flavours.

Things proceeded thus until the moment the DJ put on *Are You Ready for the Sex Girls?* by the Gleaming Spires, an early production by noted producer Shep Pettibone on the sometimes highly-regarded Posh Boy label out of San Francisco. And ready or not, here they came indeed: the entire FOXy staff, cast from the same mould but with their slight variations emphasised by their differing garb. Relative to non-Org females, clothing played little part in their everyday lives, and they were consequently inexperienced in exercising their imaginations in couturiesqe directions, tending to take literally what they read or saw. Here at The Org most of our reading and viewing matter tended towards the erotocentric and consequently their costumes presented an overview of the fetishes of the world outside, rendered more poignant since it was a world they had never known. Thus we had an emphasis on nurses, nuns, policewomen, schoolgirls, nazi officerettes, shepherdesses and so on.

The FOXes assembled informally by the buffet table and chatted and giggled. I noticed that none of them was drinking and assumed this was due to some kind of technical incompatibility with alcohol. After a while a trio of bold technicians went over and split off a couple, destabilising the intrinsic coherence of the group and causing it to disintegrate.

Just then #579 blundered over to me.

"How's it going, mate?" he went, as I had suspected, he was slightly the worse for wear, "you and me, eh? How about it? Where's my fucking beer gone?" he went, then went.

I fired up a pre-skinned splifter and the pungent aroma of hashish worked its customary chick-magnet magic and attracted the attention of a buxom police-lady and a nun (in red high-heels).

"Now, you're not going to keep that all to yourself, are you? That wouldn't be very sociable..." went the rozzette, pneumatically, "You can call me 'FOX(X), and this is my close friend FOX(Y)."

I hoped that before the evening was out I might persuade the two ladies to demonstrate precisely how close their friendship was, and I figured that Mary Jane wouldn't stand in the way so took a long drag and passing it on.

"There's no FUCKING BEER LEFT!" went #579, returning and brandishing a drained tinny. Instinctively sensing the most critical point of any party.

"Needs must when the Devil drives..." went the chick in the habit, about to prove herself uninhibited. Her eyes took on a weird look as she spontaneously started to raise her skirt, revealing shapely satin-sheaved ankles, calves, knees and thighs.

The hem continued to rise past the top of the stocking, ever-so-slowly revealing the golden fleece to our lusty gaze. Bundling the balance of her habit in one hand, she rested her left leg on a chair and flexed the right away from it, thus separating her thighs. Then, taking a goblet with her right hand, she closed her eyes to concentrate and the piss came down like the shower of gold that Zeus must have looked like to Danäe. It took a moment for her to locate the goblet and the initial spurt dribbled down her fingers and off tapered nails, but when she'd filled it she carefully set down the glass and we watched abacktaken as she filled three more with the pale yellow and mildly effervescent liquid.

"Ladies first..." went the FOX(X) and picked up a glass, she sniffed the bouquet before taking a hearty swig, and swished the liquid around her mouth to savour the flavour. "Mmmm, delicious, try some..."

#579 was desperate for grog and would've sunk virtually anything, he grabbed a glass and greedily quaffed the lot then belched indecorously. I was no stranger to the golden elixir and what prudence I possessed was quashed with the first taste, for her pish was delish.

"Drinking piss really gets me horny," went FOX(X), "It's kinda mystical, gives me an epiphany just to think about it."

"?" we went collectively.

"Firstly. On one level, when you piss it connects you with nature." She elaborated, "It's the human component of the precipitation cycle. You drink, with your mouth, obviously, and the liquid works through your system and out of your urethra then it goes through the toilet, round the U-bend down the drain, through the sewers into the sewage works and into the ocean. Where it evaporates, forms clouds, they reach a critical point where rain is produced. It fills the reservoirs which we drink from, and so the eternal circle completes itself."

"Maybe this is why Reich's research led him where it did, he started off studying sex under Freud and ended up busting clouds in the American mid-west. Maybe there's just not that much difference..." I went, lucidly.

"Pee is for precipitation, we can dig it... You and urethra. Hehehehe", the presence of #579 was starting to irk.

"But on a psychological level, the ocean is the symbol of the unconscious." FOX(X) continued, "The urinary apparatus is your link to this chain and your organ of physical communion with the symbol of the unconscious."

"But surely," I countered, "When you drink piss you break the chain, like a tape-delay copycat unit or something, and this throws things into disharmony. Negative feedback and stuff. You know."

"You might think so, but there are no contradictions in nature."

"You know what I think," went #579, momentarily coherent, "I think that the fundamental difference between the sexes is that women can't make like hosepipes when they wanna piss. They can't work out their aggression by... uh... I mean I really dig it when there's loads of butts in the urinal, then I can make like a Stuka strafing convoys of refugees. Fabtastic!"

"And what do you say, sister?" I asked.

She demurely put down her own glass, the rim was red with lipstick. "I am reminded of the words of St. Matthew*." she went, knowledgably.

I noticed that we seemed to have started a bit of a craze: around the room brazen strumbots were dropping underwear of every description and squatting over glasses, cups, punch bowls, mouths, hats, etc. The Function Room was fast turning into a Bodily Function Room. A gang of burly technicians were fighting each other to get their heads between the parted thighs of a chick who was naked but for a bikini top. Laughing heartily, the amazon straddled the brawl and emptied her full bladder into their collective upturned faces, the blokes' heads collided with a satisfyingly loud knock as they struggled to get beneath the golden jet, which seemed to stream for an inordinate time.

"What exactly is in that piss?" I asked, slightly giddy. "what've you been drinking?"

"Nothing but the finest Champagne." she went.

---



Matthew xv, 17-20 states:

...whatsoever entereth in at the mouth goeth into the belly, and is cast out into the draught. But those things which proceed out of the mouth come forth from the heart; and they defile the man. For out of the heart proceed evil thoughts, murders, adulteries, fornications, thefts, false witness, blasphemies. These are the things which defile a man: but to eat with unwashen hands defileth not a man.

"Hmmm..." I went, "Any danger of a refill?"

"Erresh, zannel fruck..." went #579, then he fell over and rolled under a table.

FOX(Y) obliged me. Now that I knew, it was obvious that the urine comprised mainly of recycled Champagne.

"So! You turn up your nose at the contents of *my* bladder?!" went FOX(X) huffily.

"No! Absolutely not..." I went, "I'd be delighted!"

"I'll bet you would!" she went, then stormed off. I made to follow her but FOX(Y) stopped me.

"I'll go," she went, "Some kind of personality profile dysfunction. She gets the monk... the hump... takes umbridge... gets offended easily but she'll be over it in a moment. You should stay and see if #579 swallows his vomit or inhales his tongue or whatever it is that you blokes are supposed to do."

I figured that would pass the time so I found the piss-head where he'd fallen and propped him up against the table.

"No digestive tract?" he went.

"Dunno." I went.

"No." He went, "That's why they never get pissed, they get all their nutrients intravenously. That's in order to simplify the analysis of stomach contents and stuff. If they've swallowed a guy's load and you find out later that you need to check it out. Every employee's jizm is logged and indexed by characteristics of sequences in its DNA. Didn't they ask you to provided a sample?"

"No."

"See. They don't have to..."

"But I don't get it. The director's daughter said she had to stay pure!"

"Yeah, that's true. The girls have to surrender all the fluids they collect on duty. Penalties for non-compliance are *very* severe. Some say too much so."

A bloke had got a FOX on the table above us. She had her legs wrapped round his waist and he was banging into her like a hydraulic ram. The air was heavy with the slap of wild bellies and the rattling of nearby plates of hors-d'oeuvres bouncing around.

"Uh turn over baby, I wanna give it you in the ass!" went the shagger, eloquently.

"Hurrr hurrr", panted the chick, "Just... gotta... make some... room... then." She extricated herself from around him and jutted her arse over the edge of the table. #579 and me paused our discussion momentarily to regard the posterior as she spread her cheeks, affording us a momentarily perfect view of her entire genitalia but I realised too late what was going to happen! An explosion of Bombay mix rained down onto the sorry drunkard's head. Upturned as it was, he coughed and spluttered beneath an avalanche of variegated titbits. I was glad it wasn't me.

"Oh sorry, I didn't know you were there" went the chick, looking over red-faced, then her partner rudely grabbed her haunches and drove his impatient member buttward.

#579 expectorated macadamias, "Yeah, sometimes they do that..." he went, "In case their date gets hungry halfway through. Saves getting up and going to the kitchen. But obviously it only works with the more durable foodstuffs. I've got to say that chocolate is especially unappetising served thus."

"I think its time you crashed mate. You're starting to cramp my style and I wanna get some of what he's got."

"What? Bombay mix?"

"Yeah, that's right."

"Uh, yeah... Feelin' kinda queasy atcherly."

I helped the tortured hack to his feet and we staggered off back to his quarters. It took him a long time to find the right key and open the door, and it took him even longer before he remembered what he'd come back for.

"Juzt ammo..." he went, flopping down into the armchair by the desk. Suddenly he belched hugely and subsequently vomited copiously over the chess game. "Phuck." he went, then reached into the disgusting orange puddle and victoriously held up Queen Justine, dripping.

"I don't remember eating this." He went, hilariously.

I manoeuvred the comic genius into the bedroom, ensacked him, then kicked him into the recovery position.

"Ahhh. You're a good mate," he went, "Cunt. I'll fucking have you when I... Just fuckin' wait, ya wanker." Then he tried to get up but the affair was bordering on tedious now so I punched him in the face and he flaked out and not a moment before time. As I tiptoed out into the dwindling night the dawn was breaking and the cock crew.

S I TIPTOED OUT into the dwindling night the dawn was breaking and the Cock Crew came round the corner in a terrible conga singing their hideous anthem.

Nah nah-nah nah-nah nah
Nah nah-nah nah-nah nah
We are the Cock Crew!

I was distracted by this shambolic spectacle and took a wrong turn on my way back to the beano and thus it was that I entered the sweet-smelling enclosure, where the stamping and snorting animals were taking that nervous repose common to their kind, I nearly turned back, debating a plan to entrap a fuck.

The cattle seemed restless, whether from fright or nervousness I could not tell, but a suspicious scrambling sound of human footsteps gave me the clue, and opening the door of her stall I came face to face with a FOX, naked and dishevelled. Immediately I assumed that some terrible misfortune had befallen her but her expression was one of such utmost guilt that her culpability could not be doubted.

"Oh, it's you. Have you come for your champers?" she went, and thus I pegged her as the aforementioned FOX(X), evidently the Peeler had peeled.

"Mmmm. Yes please!"

I lay down on the straw while the girl squatted over me and released an elegant trickle square into my mouth at just the right rate for me to swallow comfortably. I was heartily impressed by her urethral control and it took a little time before I noted that her urine tasted quite different than her friend's had. Slightly bitter, smoky, but very palatable.

"Enough?" she went.

I gurgled an affirmative and she stopped.

"Yours tastes different." I went.

"Err... another vintage, I guess." She seemed evasive.

Suddenly the "nun" came over. She was naked now too, which made her no longer a "nun". She was now a non-nun. She crushed me to her nudity in a languid and passionate kiss, I tasted the anonymous semen of an earlier encounter in her saliva, then I felt it soaking through my shirt.

"Fuck! my new Van Heusen!" I went, pulling away dismayed, "Does this shit stain?" I could really see myself explaining this at the bundle-drop.

"Do you think we're evil?" went FOX(X).

"Yeah! When the sister here fucks my new hundred buck shirt. Fucking A!"

"Do you want to punish me?" she suggested hopefully.

"It was an end of line thang, they don't make them any more... I'm fucking gutted!"

FOX(Y) looked upset and I didn't know whether it was some kind of unspecified sex-shame or guilt about fucking my shirt or any combination of the preceding.

"Let's get you cleaned up," suggested FOX(X), laying her friend down on a handy hay-bale. She delicately commenced licking the traces of semen from the girl's throat. FOX(Y) began to brighten as FOX(X) moved down to her breasts, paying inordinate attention to the nipples which didn't appear sullied. As she progressed downward she left a damp trail of saliva, which she carefully dried off with her long blond hair.

"Fuck me." went FOX(X), looking up at me momentarily as she reached FOX(Y)'s cunt.

I was happy to oblige and got naked ASAP, and my cock burst out my trousers like the alien out of John Hurt's gut in the breakfast bit from *Alien*, only not quite so horrifying. Oh I dunno.

FOX(X)'s cunt was directly over FOX(Y)'s mouth and as I menaced her labia with my best leg of three, she snapped playfully upward to lick my balls and arsehole. FOX(X) was very wet and I banged it in with such force that her gasp into FOX(Y)'s muff was muffled by the squelch. In a heightened state of arousal such as I was I proceeded with slow strokes, the better to delay my climax. My penis swelled with each stroke and as I savoured the delicious sensations I became aware of the gentle pressure of FOX(Y)'s mouth on my scrotum as she divided her attentions between the two of us. I raised myself up and observed the rapturous expression on FOX(X)'s face as she attended FOX(Y)'s cunt. FOX(Y) grunted beneath us and spread her legs to their full extent to afford better access, and FOX(X) obligingly drove deeper into her sex with her tongue, obscuring her face. I looked down toward my sex, slick with FOX(X)'s manifest-desire, as I pistoned in and out of her I could see FOX(Y)'s face bore similar expression, her eyes were closed and her lips and tongue perfectly complemented our two fucking sexes.

What a brief time is allotted man! Despite my deepest desire to prolong the session, the sight of those beatific countenances was too much and I felt my scrotum tighten and those treacherous muscles start to work. I shot the first bolt square into FOX(X)'s womb, but FOX(Y)'s teeth gently pulled at my scrotum, and withdrew my shaft out and the second bolt shot into the air and spattered into the valley of FOX(X)'s arse, just above her anus. FOX(Y) had me in her mouth before I was spent though, my shaft embedded in her throat, and the balance must have shot directly down to her stomach. I moved aside and allowed FOX(Y) to conscientiously clean up the valley of FOX(X)'s arse, with particular regard to her anus, FOX(X) relaxed her sphincter and allowed access to FOX(Y)'s eager tongue. Her rump quivered deliciously as the waves of ecstasy swept over her.

Afterwards we lay in the hay in a post-coital situation and I retrieved an emergency doobie from my trousers. I lit up and it may have been the severity of the fire-risk which prompted me to say to FOX(X) "You're not a FOX, are you?"

"Uh? What? What makes you say that?"

"Your piss tasted different. For one thing. It was the real thing, wasn't it? Piss. I mean."

"Straight up? I actually am the Director's daughter. It was my DNA he scanned for the FOX prototypes. Hence the resemblance. Sometimes I wish I was a FOX though..."

"It must be a simple life..."

"Spot on!" went FOX(Y), "but not because our lives are any simpler, we're just brainier."

"That's what I mean," went FOX(X).

"Well, this has all been very... illuminating... but I'd better be getting back to the action. Need a brew, you dig?" I went, ungraciously.

The girls declined, they both looked like they needed to go and recharge their batteries. Not to imply that I'm a stud or anything, since they had started before me, and in grand style I may add.

When I got back to the party it was crap. The technicians had started playing Blind Man's Muff, where a blindfolded contestant identifies a FOX by the taste of their secretion. I was informed by a rather tiresome spectator that the differences are very subtle, being dependant on lubrication levels and so on, and a great deal of expertise is called for. It made for mediocre entertainment to start with, but the final round was enlivened by accusations of pig-sucking (ie excessive salivation on the contestants' parts) and poor sportsmanship prevailed, the ensuing fisticuffs curtailing the event with no clear victor. That was a shame because the prize was pretty good, a Polaroid of the Director in flagranté with a mystery animal, vegetable and mineral simultaneously, but no doubt it would be reproduced in the next issue of *The Organ.* One by one the chicks were going flat in direct relation to the party, so I went back to my room to crash. The wind was rushing in off the desert and outside my window any last stray noise from the party was drowned by the song of the aerial farm.

ROUND DINNERTIME I was roused to consciousness by the rude jangle of the videophone on the night table. It was the Director, in urgent tones he told me to meet him immediately, in the canteen, at once. I did a condensed version of my usual morning stuff and got there just as he was just polishing off his Weet-Bix with Milk of Magnesia.

"Have I got time for a spot..." I went.

"No no no!" he masticated, "This is a terrible business! Come with me m'boy!" I was distinctly unsettled by his sudden informal appellation but I recognised #579's' quarters as soon as we got to them

"Brace yerself!" went the Director, as he waved aside a couple of uniformed Org guards, "It's not a pretty sight!"

The room was in darkness, but as my pupils dilated I made out a weird silhouette dangling from the light socket. The Director flicked the switch and as the current flowed the dangling figure buzzed and twitched on the cord like some sort of spastic.

"Bugger!" went the Director. I turned on the angle-poise lamp on the desk and angle-poised it.

"I'm always doing that." went the Director worryingly.

The figure was wearing a black satin camisole and fishnet stockings, and a gas mask. The hose was connected to an industrial sized four-gallon can of polystyrene cement, aeroplane glue. As the dangly corpse slowly rotated in the slight breeze I saw that the teddy was unfastened at the crotch and a huge dildo protruded from its anus, then I noticed the wedding tackle, erect in a death-spasm.

"It's a bloke!" I went, observantly.

"Well, get 'im down!"

I got a chair and stood on it. It took a couple of seconds with my Swiss Army knife to cut through the electrical cord that suspended the figure. As I cut the support the body dropped unceremoniously to the floor with a loud noise.

"Should've checked if he was still alive." went the Director, "Still, never mind." and so saying, he pulled the mask off the face. It came as no surprise to find this was the corpse of #579. The first thing I noticed was the bloated purple tongue stuck out from an enormous smile. Then the Director pulled the dildo out of the corpse's arse, there was a vile sucking noise and a horrendous terminal fart. He brandished the strange instrument dangerously toward me.

"Hmmm..." I went, thoughtfully "the dildo is *exactly* the same shape as his penis! It must have been made from a cast of it."

"Exactly! Notice anything else?"

"It's smeared with shit and stuff."

"Underneath that."

"Oh yeah... It seems to be papier-maché, but that's not newsprint, but you can make out words..."

"...wet lips; into her twitching sheath... suddenly neglected phallus vomited its warm cream on... double fold of flesh and into her open cunt... pissed all over her midriff, an evil-smelling liquid... these are all bits from *Rape vs. Murder*!"

"He fucked himself with his own book! What a fucking wanker!"

"It's worse than that! Look!"

On the desk was a copy of the MS of *Rape vs. Murder*, the terminal spending had pooled upon it copiously and soaked into the paper, drying to a crusty horrible mess. Then the Director cursed as he trod on some broken glass. He gingerly picked up a piece of crystal, then examined the desk.

"There's no glass here, but there are traces of liquid. The glass must have been knocked over, spilled its charge and rolled onto the floor, where it broke. The manuscript also appears to have absorbed most of the liquid... Any ideas?"

I sniffed the MS, "Smells like piss, but its hard to tell with all that encrusted jizz. And he may have emptied his bladder at the moment of death, he'd been liberally partaking of the old FOX-piss at the bash."

"Hmm..." continued the Director, "Hey look! Evidence!" he held up an elegant woman's shoe. The murderess!"

I identified the patent leather stiletto immediately, "It belongs to your daughter."

"Uh, better get her in here for a chat." He picked up the phone and called her up, she arrived within a couple of minutes. I experienced some difficulty meeting her gaze after our intimacies of the previous evening.

"Yes, I did come here, when I stormed off, you remember" she went, "I knew you'd bring him here and I wanted to exploit the... uh victim's inebriation to try and blag a proof copy of his book."

"And when he wouldn't come through, you lost control of your latent bibliomania and ruthlessly expired him, and then set it up to look like... a hideous accident!"

"No, I couldn't have! Haven't you heard of Asimov's Laws? The first one says that a robot must never harm a human!"

"Aha!" I went, "You're forgetting! I know your little secret!"

"Eh, what?" went the Director.

"Oh, no, I really am a FOX. That was just a wind-up."

"And the taste of your piss? How do you explain that?"

"My piss tasted like piss because it *was* piss, just not my piss. Well it was my piss then, but before that it was someone else's."

"#579s'." we went, simultaneously.

"Urrrgh!! You mean to say? I drank ANOTHER BLOKE'S PISS!! URRRGHH! FUCK! PFT PFT!"

I nipped out for quick spew, and when I got back it was time for the thrilling denouement.

"It was all an accident, honest!" went the Director's daughter, starting to lose her characteristic composure, "when he wouldn't come through with the proof I tried him with a spot of the old urinology/auto-asphyxiation kick. His needs were... *strange*. He was jaded as all fuck, 'wanker's block' he called it. He found his work was totally draining his sexual potency and needed to work himself into an erotic frenzy to be inspired to proceed with his book. Then he would use his book to arouse him so he could work on the subsequent draft. But the feedback loop was closing and the resultant sex-karma probably caused him to *reverse his own orgonic current against the flow of the sex/time continuum* and that is probably was what killed him."

"But I thought he'd finished the book this very evening? Wasn't that what the party was for?"

"What can I say? He was devoted to his work. But look on the bright side, we now have the perfect opportunity to check out that necrophile kick that everyone raves about."

"Well, I guess that just about wraps it up then... except..." went the Director, "...for one final mystery. I wonder who punched the poor chap in the clock? I could barely get the mask off over that shiner!"

"Errr..." I went.

# III

# The Love that Cannot Pronounce its Name

Non, dis-je. Ce n'était pas pour nous amuser,
c'était pour ton instruction, que nous sommes
venus sur l'éboulis. Tu sauras, maintenant, ce que
c'est que la marée.

— *André Pieyre de Mandiargues*

Quand B fit l'amour avec A
Les paragraphes s'embrassèrent
Les virgules s'avancèrent
Tendant leur cou par-dessus les ponts de fer
Et l'alphabet blessé za mort
S'évanouit dans les bras d'une interrogation
muette

— *Raymond Queneau*

E GOT SHUT OF #579 at midnight, and the entire staff drove out to the desert cemetery. The Director's Duesenberg led the convoy, then came the funereal black missile-launcher flanked by six outriders, and we brought up the rear, a bus-load of groggy dishevelled techies and the FOXes, sobbing but sexy as fuck in their black mourning kit, and a sombre crew too we were.

No grave had been excavated in the dusty red earth with a JCB or anything like that. It wouldn't be necessary, because #579 was being disposed of with full honours in the guided-missile burial that was traditional, and to my knowledge unique, to prominent members of The Org.

We all got out of the bus and picked up a stubby from the driver's esky on the way out. Then we stood drinking around for a bit while the missile-launcher got into position. Someone produced a ghettoblaster and soon it was blaring out Alternative TV's anthemic *Love Lies Limp.* #579 would habitually endorse virtually any tune he heard by demanding it be played at his funeral, and this was merely the most recent nominee. He had been very careful to specify the BBC John Peel Show version, wherein all the expletives were obscured by the honking of an old-fashioned car-horn.

One of the FOXes had been nominated to deliver a eulogy. Her voice was cracking with emotion as she read one of the dead writer's favourite poems. It was "On The Medusa of Leonardo Da Vinci in the Florentine Gallery" written in the 19th century by notorious party animal Percy Shelley:

> It lieth, gazing on the midnight sky,
> Upon the cloudy mountain-peak supine;
> Below, far lands are seen tremblingly;
> Its horror and its beauty are divine.
> Upon its lips and eyelids seem to lie
> Loveliness like a shadow, from which shine,
> Fiery and lurid, struggling underneath,
> The agonies of anguish and of death.
>
> Yet it is less the horror than the grace
> Which turns the gazer's spirit into stone,
> Whereon the lineaments of that dead face
> Are graven, till the characters be grown
> Into itself, and thought no more can trace;
> 'Tis the melodious hue of beauty thrown
> Athwart the darkness and the glare of pain
> Which humanize and harmonize the strain.
>
> And from its head as from one body grow,
> As          grass out of a watery rock,
> Hairs which are vipers, and they curl and flow
> And their long tangles in each other lock,
> And with their unending involutions show
> Their mailèd radiance, as it were to mock
> The torture and the death within, and saw
> The solid air with many a raggèd jaw.

And, from a stone beside, a poisonous eft
Peeps idly into those Gorgonian eyes;
Whilst in the air a ghastly bat, bereft
Of sense, has flitted with a mad surprise
Out of the cave this hideous light had cleft,
And he comes hastening like a moth that hies
After a taper; and the midnight sky
Flares, a light more dread than obscurity.

'Tis the tempestuous loveliness of terror;
For from the serpents gleams a brazen glare
Kindled by that inexorable error,
Which makes a thrilling vapour of the air
Becomes a          and ever-shifting mirror
Of all the beauty and the terror there-
A woman's countenance, with serpent-locks,
Gazing in death on Heaven from those wet rocks.

Most of the mourners had lost interest in the course of the long poem and had used the time to get pleasantly lagered up. The Director read a rather moving tribute of his own composition:

#579 was thick
and now #579 is dead.
He thought with his dick
and it fucked with his head.

There were mumbles of approval. A general hubbub was commencing and the sense of anticipation was tangible. The uniformed outriders, scary in their grey leathers, formed a guard of honour shouldering rifles that I hadn't previously noticed.

The commander of the party removed the Australian flag* from the missile and a solitary bu(n)gler played the last post really badly as the gantry hummed and elevated the missile into the vertical firing position. The moment it hit 90° there was a blaze of gunfire, the engines ignited and the rocket rose into the night sky more slowly than looked safe, even for a missile, taking #579 on his last journey.

We were distracted for a moment by one of The Org's pilots who was paying his personal tribute in skywriting overhead: "579 r-i-d". The stupid fucker

---

* The precursor to the modern flag was the vexilloid, a pole topped with an emblem, termed a finial, that represented the group's collective identity. These generally symbolised rulers or gods, and featured carved totemic animals such as Anubis the Egyptian jackal, the Chinese phoenix, aquila the Roman eagle, the white horse of the Angles and Saxons, or wolves and boars. Also common were wreaths of honour, crescents, metal vanes, fans, feathers and portraits. The finial was often adorned with animal tails or strips of cloth and it is from these that the modern flag is thought to have originated, the finial now being usually manifested as a simple point or button.

It is generally accepted that the vexilloid was a development of the phallic object as represented in totem poles, maypoles, and so on. This analogy brings us to the conclusion that if the pole is equivalent to the shaft of the penis, then the finial's counterpart is the glans of the penis, and the flag is thus symbolic of the ejaculatory issue of the penis.

It is tempting to further extrapolate the field of the flag as correspondent to the seminal fluid, and its devices to the spermatozoa.

was suffering from alcohol-induced dyslexia and had rotated the terminal "p" by 180°. Still, it was the thought that counted, and the luminous green smoke he'd used looked way spooky nevertheless. I was glad the pilot gave the missile a wide berth, because when it had reached a preordained height there was a blinding flash of light and a huge cheer went up from the crowd, merging into the ear-splitting soundwave moments later. I quickly gathered that the explosion was part of the ceremony, and #579's mortal remains had been agreeably atomised.

A pissed geezer in a vicar's outfit pushed his way towards the front of the throng. "Ashes to Ashes, dust to dust, when you go to the khazi, remember to flush."

"Amen." went we all.

"Rot quick, old pal!"

Everyone got back in the bus and I was sat next to a technician. We all knew that we were obliged to recommence the party when we got back to the Org, that was what he would have wanted. The evening was quite warm and I opened the window and someone pushed a tape in the ghettoblaster, it was The Eyes doing *When the Night Falls* and we dug it.

"So, this bloke, he was a writer was he?" asked the technician sitting next to me.

"Yeah."

## "So he must have written porn˙ if he worked here?"

---

Pornography is the oldest literature in the world, and there is good cause to believe that it must be the first genre of any kind; since theatre is the oldest of art forms, and it would not seem unreasonable to assume that the most primitive theatre consisted of sexual spectacle.

The word "pornography" itself originated as recently as the mid-nineteenth century, referring to descriptions of the life and activities of prostitutes. It soon came to mean the explicit description or exhibition of sexual subjects or activity in a manner intended to stimulate erotic rather than aesthetic responses.

The word is a compound of the Greek words *porne* (a prostitute) and *graphein* (here taken to mean writing). Of course, the word "graphic" has many meanings: anything drawn with a pencil or pen; pertaining to handwriting, diagrams, graphs, or similar figures, drawing, painting, engraving, etching, etc.; relating to or producing any kind of pictorial representations; or producing with words the effect of a clear pictorial representation, vividly descriptive, conveying all details, especially unpleasant or unwelcome ones.

It is generally accepted that our modern Roman alphabet derived via the Etruscan from the Greek, which in its turn had developed from the Phoenician, the first consonantal alphabet. It was the Phoenicians who had made the quantum leap from the pictograms of ancient Egypt by the process of phonetization, the association of sounds with symbols. Thus, for example, the ideograms for Semitic beth (house), gimel (camel), and daleth (door) became associated by the principle of acrophony with their initial sounds as uttered in speech (ie "b", "g" and "d"). The Phoenicians used 22 of the several hundred of Egyptian hieroglyphics, and the ultimately pictographic origin of the characters is revealed by the names of the letters themselves. The Phoenician word "aleph" (in

Greek "alpha") meaning ox or beef, the Phoenician word "beth" (in Greek "beta") meaning house. The word alphabet, which is documented from the 3<sup>rd</sup> century BC, literally meaning "cowshed".

The actual cause of the development of the alphabet remains one of the greatest mysteries of history. It has been suggested that the impetus was provided by the desire to permanently record the poetry of Homer, but this is uncorroborated.

In antiquity authors had no lack of terms for the genital organs of either sex, but here we are concerned with the implications of just two: the designation of the female sexual organ by the Greek letter Lambda, "Λ" (the equivalent of "L" in the later Roman alphabet that we use), and to the designation of the male sexual organ by the Greek Iota longum (their name for the letter "I" which is unchanged in our alphabet).

This idea of the representation of the genitals by letters occurs in the Priapeia. These short and jocular Latin epigrams adorned statues of Priapus, Roman god of fertility and have been attributed with varying degrees of reliability to the greatest of classical poets, including Martial, Petronius, Catullus, Ovid, Tibullus and Cinna. Of interest here is the epigram numbered 54:

ED si scribas temonemque insuper addas,
  qui medium vult te scindere, pictus erit.

That is to say: if you write the letters E and D and place a dash between them thus: E—D, you have a representation of a penis that wishes to cleave through the middle of "D", which represents an anus to be cleaved. The ambiguity arises from writing the phonetically equivalent letter "D" instead of the Latin word "te", meaning thee. The shape of the penis is not immediately apparent, but the top and bottom strokes of the letter E may be taken as forming the testicles whilst the middle stroke, continued by the dash, represents the shaft of the penis.

Several centuries separate the authors of the *Priapeia* from the American Intellectual Susan Sontag, but in a famous essay she comments thus on Pauline Réage's *The Story of O*:

> O's quest is neatly summed up in the expressive letter which serves her for a name. "O" suggests a cartoon of her sex, not her individual sex but simply woman; it also stands for a nothing. But what Story of O unfolds is a spiritual paradox, that of the full void and of the vacuity that is also a plenum. The power of the book lies exactly in the anguish stirred up by the continuing presence of this paradox.

Réage herself dismissed the cartoon-sex hypothesis and stated that O's name was merely a representation of zero, the absence of self that was her heroine's psychic destination. But even if unintentional, one cannot help but consider the alternative more resonant, since this would transform the letter "I" into a cartoon of a phallus, and consequently render any first person narrative latently pornographic.

If we follow this line of reasoning to its logical conclusion, we find that each individual letter of our alphabet may become a pictogram that represents a component of a sexual act.

Thus on a simple pictorial level, the letter "A" could signify for example an erect penis, based on a top or side elevation. "B" could signify a pair of breasts based on a top elevation. It is tempting to assign genital properties to the vowels and secondary erogenous or fetishistic properties to the consonants.

The system can be elaborated by admitting abstract concepts. Thus, "I" could signify a generic penetrator, and "O" a generic orifice. Letters could also be derived from

"So I gather."

"Was it any good? You know... Phwoar! Eh?"

"Well, I nicked a copy of his last book from the scene of the crime, but the pages were... all... uh... stuck together. And when I tried to prise them apart their surfaces separated – surprisingly uniformly. I was left with a book comprising entirely of blank leaves."

The technician sniggered, "What was he called?"

"*The Enormous Sextet.*"

"Uh, you what? I said, what was *he* called, the bloke?"

I said I didn't know and looked out of the window. The fucked up skywriting was just starting to break up in the still night, drifting away, superimposed on the ancient scribbling of the constellations. The sky was thick with stars and I wondered how many of them were already dead, squirting the dregs of their light

---

compounds of others: "J" could signify an ejaculating "I", and "Q", a lubricating "O". "J" and "Q" could then be further abstracted to signify the secretions themselves rather than the organs of their production. (In French, the letter "Q" especially invites visual and phonetic mimology, associating as it does with "cul", colloquially arse or cunt.)

Taking this concept one stage further, each word becomes combination of components forming an instance of an act and a succession of acts forms a sentence. The conclusion is as inescapable as it is staggering in its implications— all writing is, literally, literally pornographic, with the "graphic" component of the word now manifesting its full range of its definitions.

toward us. Maybe all of them were. Fuck knew, but I took comfort from the idea that it was statistically unlikely. Maybe a few of them were croaking while I looked. I was sure I could see them obligingly winking out. They would have blown up eons ago though, long before I'd taken up my telescope, or even thought about the stars, or been born, or before my parents had been born etc. But what was the life cycle of stars? I couldn't remember how long they were supposed to last. Or how often they died. Just the once I guessed. I know they last a long time and there's a lot of them, so no dearth impends. But what about the constellations? It only took one of component to expire and the symbols were altered substantially. Time would rewrite the vocabulary of the spheres and all the old legends would be obsolete. What would supersede them?

Hove, May 14th 1995
— Melbourne, January 1st 1997

Alternative TV. *The Peel Sessions.* CD. Newcastle: Overground Records, c1995.

Asimov, Isaac. *I, Robot.* New York: Gnome, 1950.

Bataille, Georges. *L'Erotisme.* Paris: Editions de Minuit, 1992, 1957.

———. *Oeuvres Completes* Paris: Gallimard, 1970-<1988>.

Bateson, Gregory. *Steps to an Ecology of Mind.* New York: Ballantine Books, 1972.

Borges, Jorge Luis, with Margarita Guerrero. *The Book of Imaginary Beings.* Trans. Norman Thomas di Giovanni in collaboration with the author. Harmondsworth: Penguin, 1974.

Borowczyk, Walerian, dir. *Ars amandi.* Perf. Marina Pierro, Michele Placido,  Massimo Girotti, et al. France/Italy, 1983.

———. *Contes Immoraux.* Perf. Charlotte Alexandra, Florence Bellamy,  Paloma Picasso, et al. France: Argos Film, 1974.

———. *Emmanuelle 5.* Perf. Dominique Gabrielle et al. France: New Horizon Picture Corp., 1987.

Campbell, George L. *Handbook of Scripts and Alphabets.* London: Routledge, 1997.

Crest, Jason. "Literary Erotica: A Tri-orthogonal Perspective." *British Journal of Experimental Literature.* 23:997-1013, 1966.

Crowley, Aleister. *The Book of Thoth : a Short Essay on the Tarot of the Egyptians.* York Beach, Maine: Weissner, 1969.

———. *Tarot Divination.* York Beach, Maine: Weissner, 1976.

Crystal, David. *The Cambridge Encyclopedia of the English Language.* Cambridge: Cambridge University Press, 1995.

Daimler, Harriet. *Darling.* Paris: Olympia, 1956.

———. *Innocence.* Paris: Olympia, 1957.

———. *The Organisation.* Paris: Olympia, 1957.

De Las Lunas, Carmencita. *Thongs.* Paris: Olympia, 1956.

Del Piombo, Akbar. *Cosimo's Wife.* Paris: Olympia, 1957.

———. *Skirts.* Paris: Olympia, 1956.

———. *The Traveller's Companion.* Paris: Olympia, 1957.

———. *Who Pushed Paula?.* Paris: Olympia, 1956.

Dick, Phillip K. *Do Androids Dream of Electric Sheep?* New York: Doubleday, 1968.

Drake, Hamilton. *Sin for Breakfast.* Paris: Olympia, 1957.

Drucker, Johanna. *The Alphabetic Labyrinth: The Letters in History and Imagination* London: Thames & Hudson, 1995.

Fleming, Ian. *Live and Let Die.* London: Cape, 1957.

Foley, Carol A. *The Australian Flag.* Sydney: Federation Press, 1996.

Foucault, Michel. *Death and the Labyrinth: The World of Raymond Roussel.* Trans. Charles Ruas. Garden City, New York: Doubleday, 1986.

Genette, Gerard. *Mimologiques: Voyage en Cratylie.* Paris: Editions du Seuil, c1976.

The Gleaming Spires. "Are You Ready for the Sex Girls?" *The Posh Boy Story.* CD. London: Damaged Goods, 1993.

Gysin, Brion. "Dream Machine." *Olympia* 2 (1962):31-32.

Hodges, Andrew. *Alan Turing: The Enigma of Intelligence.* London: Unwin Paperbacks, 1985.

Homer & Associates. *A Bedside Odyssey.* Paris: Olympia, 1962.

Jacobs, Carol. "On Looking at Shelley's Medusa." *Yale French Studies* 69 (1985):163-79.

Kearney, Patrick J. *A History of Erotic Literature.* London: Macmillan, 1982.

———. *The Paris Olympia Press.* London: Black Spring Press, 1987.

*Las Vegas Grind* [four volumes] LP record. Strip Records, c1986-92.

Lautreamont, Comte de. *Oeuvres completes [de] Lautreamont [et de] Germain Nouveau.* Textes etablis, presentes et annotes par Pierre-Olivier Walzer. Paris: Gallimard, 1970.

Lem, Stanislaw. *The Cyberiad: Fables for the Cybernetic Age.* Trans Michael Kandel. New York: Seabury, 1974.

Lengel, Frances. *Helen and Desire.* Paris: Olympia, 1956.

———. *School for Sin.* Paris: Olympia, 1955.

———. *White Thighs.* Paris: Olympia, 1955.

Mardaan, Ataullah. *Deva-Dasi.* Paris: Olympia, 1957.

———. *Kama Houri.* Paris: Olympia, 1956.

Martin, Ed. *Busy Bodies.* Paris: Olympia, 1963.

———. *Frankenstein '69.* New York: Olympia, 1969.

Parker, W.H. (ed. trans.). *Priapea: Poems for a Phallic God.* London: Croom Helm, 1988.

Paré, Ambroise. *The Collected Works of Ambroise Paré.* Facsimile of 1634 ed. Trans. Thomas Johnson. Pound Ridge, New York: Milford House, 1968.

Perez, Faustino. *Until She Screams.* Paris: Olympia, 1956.

Perkins, Michael. *The Secret Record.: Modern Erotic Literature.* New York: Morrow, 1976.

Pickover, Clifford A. *Computers and the Imagination: Visual Adventures Beyond the Edge.* New York: St. Martin's Press, 1991.

Pierre, Jose (ed.). *Investigating Sex: Surrealist Research, 1928-1932.* Trans. Malcolm Imrie. London; New York: Verso, 1992.

Pieyre de Mandiargues, Andre. "La Marée." In *Mascarets.* Paris: Gallimard, 1990.

Potter, Simeon. *Our Language.* Harmondsworth: Penguin, 1950.

Praz, Mario. *The Romantic Agony.* New York: Meridian, 1956.

Queneau, Raymond. *Raymond Queneau: Unicorn French Series.* vol. 11. Trans. Teo Savory. Santa Barbara: Unicorn Press, 1971.

The Red Crayola with the Familiar Ugly. *The Parable of Arable Land.* LP record. Houston: International Artists, 1967.

Richardson, Humphrey. *The Sexual Life of Robinson Crusoe.* Paris: Olympia, 1955.

Robbe-Grillet, Alain, dir. *Trans Europ Express.* Perf. Charles Millot , Marie-France Pisier, Alain Robbe-Grillet, Jean-Louis Trintignant, et al. France: Como Film Production, 1966.

———. *Glissements Progressifs du Plaisir.* Paris: Editions de Minuit, 1973.

———. *Le Maison de Rendez-Vous.* Paris: Editions de Minuit, 1965.

Roussel, Raymond. *How I Wrote Certain of my Books.* New York: Exact Change, 1995.

———. *Oeuvres.* Paris: Pauvert, 1994-<c1998>.

Sampson, Geoffrey. *Writing Systems: a Linguistic Introduction.* London: Hutchinson, 1985.

Scott, George Ryley. *Scott's Encyclopedia of Sex.* London: T. Werner Laurie, 1939.

Searle, John R. "Minds, Brains, and Programs." In *The Behavioural and Brain Sciences.* vol. 3. Cambridge: Cambridge University Press, 1980.

Smithers, L.C., and Sir Richard Burton. *Priapiea* London: Erotika Biblion Soc., 1889.

Sommerville, Ian. "Flicker." *Olympia* 2 (1962):32-37.

Sontag, Susan. "The Pornographic Imagination." In *Styles of Radical Will.* New York: Farrar, Straus and Giroux, 1966.

Strong, Simon. "Boredom." In *Suspect Device.* Ed. Stewart Home. London: Serpent's Tail, 1999.

Tohill, Cathal, and Pete Tombs. *Immoral Tales: Sex and Horror Cinema in Europe, 1956-1984.* London: Primitive Press, 1994.

Turing, Alan. "Computing Machinery and Intelligence." *Mind.* Vol. LIX, no. 236 (October 1950).

Vonnegut Jr., Kurt. "The Big Space Fuck." In *Again, Dangerous Visions*. Ed. Harlan Ellison. New York: Doubleday, 1972.

Walter, W. Grey. *The Living Brain*. London: Duckworth, 1953.

White, T.H (ed., trans.). *The Book of Beasts; Being a Translation from a Latin Bestiary of the Twelfth Century*. London: Cape, 1954.

Wilkins, A., Nimmo-Smith, I., Tait, A., McManus, C., Sala, S., Tilley, A., Arnold, K., Barrie, M., Scott, S. "A Neurological Basis for Visual Discomfort." In *Brain* 107 (1984): 989-1017.

Williams, Linda. *Hard Core: Power, Pleasure, and the "Frenzy of the Visible."* London: Pandora Press, 1990.

*

# AUTHOR'S NOTE

I started writing *66mindfuck99* on the morning of Monday 14 May 1995 in the luxurious basement flat of 11 Hamilton Mansions, Fourth Avenue, Hove, just off the seafront. I was using Word 6.0 on my Gateway 2000 HandBook 486 and had some Fiona Cooper softcore videos playing on mute on the VHS accompanied by various GG Allin albums, a bootleg of Nirvana's final broadcast from Rome on 23 February 1994, and *Hen's Teeth Volume One*, one of the first and greatest English psyche rarities comp CDs. Over the next three weeks I knocked out around half of the first complete draft but then I decided to emigrate to Australia and any further development was delayed.

At a loose end in a strange country on New Year's Eve I decided to knock the thing over shortly after midnight. It was still 1996 in the UK and I worked on until 2:20AM when all of the essential material appeared extant. On completion of this first draft I was listening to the Butthole Surfers' *Electriclarryland* and lots of Robyn Hitchcock discs.

The manuscript remained unpublished until May 2005 when I celebrated ten years since completion and privately issued it in a hors commers edition of fifty. Most of them are still under my bed.

The head of the Copyright and Intellectual Property Enforcement Squad wants his top agent sacked, or put behind a desk. Instead the body count keeps rising because The Bastardizer is 100% obsessed with dishing out street justice on behalf of the music industry. Rules, like bones, were made to be broken. The Bastardizer did not care who got in his way. If they pissed him off he wiped them out!

The Bastardizer had a feeling for violence. That was what compelled him to cripple, maim and murder all those who didn't worship at the altar of the Berne Convention of 1886 and the Paris Act of 1971. The thud of his fist on a copyright infringer's face did something for his soul. The thud of a boot in their groin did more! Pumping copyright violators full of lead was even better... guilty or not he wanted them dead!

What no one could have foreseen was The Bastardizer's chance encounter (on an operating table of all places) with a geriatric pornographer. This caused the story to morph messily into forms of literary experimentation that put the music industry and the book world into a tailspin...

**A BOOK THAT VANISHED UP ITS OWN ARSE AND CAME BACK TO TELL THE TALE!**

TITLE: THE BASTARDIZER POLISHES A TURD
AUTHOR: CHUS MARTINEZ
ILLUSTRATED BY SONKE RICKERTSEN
INTRODUCTION BY STEWART HOME
Cripplegate Books, London. October 2022
Paperback / 158 pages / illustrated / 9781838218942

# DENIZEN OF THE DEAD

**THE HORRORS OF CLARENDON COURT**
**EDITED BY STEWART HOME**

— WARNING! —

You are about to enter the City of London,
the most evil and corrupt place on the planet!

On the border between the City's Cripplegate ward and south Islington's Bone Hill district stands Clarendon Court AKA The Denizen - an elite and newly built luxury apartment block of 99 flats marketed to property investors.

Exclusive? Yes.
Reassuringly expensive? Yes.
Safe? Undoubtedly not!

There were stories, just rumours, about what went on there. Rumours about perversion, orgies, ghosts, bad feng shui and shockingly unpleasant deaths.

When a gorgeous young nymphomaniac bursts into a Clarendon Court apartment, the whole story of depravity and corruption is revealed.

In this collection of short fiction by today's top writers the Clarendon Court investment flats really are haunted by the ghosts of Cripplegate's wild past, when the hood was notorious for its brothels and the ultra-violent criminals who frequented them.

On top of this there's a problem with the spirits of hundreds of thousands of unhappy souls whose corpses were dumped in both local plague pits and the more recent Golden Lane mega-morgue, a huge Victorian Palace of the Dead.

This anthology is a protest against property speculation and a new take on the genre of haunted house horror fiction. The book itself is a talisman that defends our communities against developers and inside it also features Spell Series by the w.o.n.d.e.r. coven. The symbols of this living spell are a lock and key designed to dismantle the neoliberal project and overdevelopment as represented by The Denizen.

Featuring work from
Paul Ewen, Tariq Goddard,
Iphgenia Baal, Chris Petit,
Steve Finbow, John King,
Chloe Aridjis, Tom McCarthy,
Liz Rever, Katrina Palmer,
Michael Hampton,
Bridget Penney,
Stewart Home
and many more!

# BARON'S COURT, ALL CHANGE

## TERRY TAYLOR

### INTRODUCED BY STEWART HOME

**Baron's Court, All Change** is the Holy Grail of beatnik novels, Terry Taylor's book documents one summer in the life of an unnamed sixteen year-old narrator. Leaving home and his job he dabbles in spiritualism, is seduced by an older woman and gets rich quick from drug dealing. This is a world of sharp suits, jazz, kicks, "spades", nightclubs and sex. A London that is already swinging half a decade before the rest of the world catches on.

Terry Taylor (1933-2014) was the much younger lover of Ida Kar, whose National Portrait Gallery collection includes a series of photographs of Terry getting stoned in London's Soho back in 1956. His proto-mod exploits as a young man are fictionalised in Colin MacInnes' famous novel *Absolute Beginners*. Throughout Taylor's life music, magic rituals and hallucinogenic drugs loomed large. Terry spent time in Goa and hung out with William Burroughs in Tangier before settling down in the wilds of north Wales, where he continued to dig modern jazz and perfect his occult practices.

2021 (originally published 1961) / 5½×8½" / 208 pp

**STEWART HOME**

This is the story of Ray "The Cat" Jones who wanted to become middleweight boxing champion of the world but eventually made his mark as the greatest cat burglar of all time.

Ray is a modern-day Robin Hood waging a relentless class war against the rich. From the jewels of movie stars Elizabeth Taylor and Sophia Loren, to the private papers of the Duke of Windsor, paintings by Rubens and Rembrandt, and the furs of the London aristocracy, Ray's carefully targeted burglaries are perfectly planned and thrillingly executed.

A vision of London's underworld from wartime to near present.

The narrative weaves between the clubs of Soho, populated by gangsters and gamblers, to the mansions of Kensington and Hampstead, inhabited by corrupt politicians and millionaires, and on into the dingy cells of the city's prisons.

2021 (originally published 2014) / 5½×8½" / 256 pp